JUDAS KILLER

Judas Killer

LAYLA M. GATLIN
Kayla N. Todd

Layla M. Gatlin & Kayla N. Todd

Prologue

The room was dark, illuminated by nothing other than the soft glow from the television set and of the moon trying to peek out from behind the pulled curtains. The news anchor was a tall man. He wore a crisp button up and tie and spoke with a soothing voice. But this voice didn't match the story it told.

The scene on the screen behind him showed several police cars with flashing lights surrounding a gas station nestled downtown. A gruff man stumbled out of the station with his hands in the air. He was drunk and his gray shirt ripping at the collar, revealing several bloody scratches on his chest. His brown hair, drenched in sweat, and his jeans appeared to be covered in oil and seemed to be missing their button. Police rushed him with guns drawn and forced him to the ground. You could see them yelling something at him, but there was no sound from the video, only the news anchor narrating. In moments, they had him handcuffed and up, being pushed towards the nearest patrol car. Another policeman opened the door, and they shoved the man inside.

The news man gestured behind him at the scene. "As you can see from the security footage, they apprehended the suspect at a gas station about three blocks from the assault. Police have confirmed that the victim has positively identified the suspect taken into custody and they are simply waiting on DNA results to confirm. They have released the names, and we are told that the victim is a 23-year-old, Katherine Hamilton, from Green Port. According to the report, she took her car in to be serviced Monday morning by a local mechanic from NYC, Steve Michaels. According to Hamilton's statement, Michaels was just closing up shop but then proceeded to invite her in, saying that he would 'take care of her'. After getting her inside the shop, he reportedly locked the door and sexually assaulted her. Hamilton fought back, eventually tearing Michaels' shirt and scratching his chest until it bled. After which she claims he fled the scene in a panic. A patron of the gas station where the officers apprehended Michaels called 911 after seeing Michaels knock the cashier over the head with a bottle and move on to steal and chug can after can of beer from the refrigerated cooler. Police say evidence on Michaels' clothes is enough for a conviction, but they are waiting to receive the DNA evidence from under Hamilton's nails before proceeding to a trial."

The TV clicks off and the solemn woman on the couch drops the remote and slowly rises to her feet. She makes her way through the darkness and up the stairs. A single teardrop staining each of the wooden steps behind her as she ascends. The door at the end of the hall creeks open and a face peers out, but the woman doesn't seem to notice. She continues to make her way slowly into another room. The door closes.

And then...

Silence.

Chapter 1

Two officers sit at the table drinking their coffee and finishing their breakfast. The first, a female named Jane Masters, looks out the window to watch all the people as they walk by. She bites into her sandwich and looks back at her partner, a ruggedly handsome man with light brown hair that's grayed at the edges from stress, named Sean Fenton.

Did they figure out who broke into the bank? She glances back out the window at the busy New York street. To her, everyone is a criminal. She thinks that all of them have broken the law at one point or another. Nobody is trustworthy. Not really. She's the type of person who has to build up trust for you in her own time. Sadly, people don't stay in her life long enough. Really, aside from her parents who live a few states away, her partner across the table is probably the person she's known the longest. And even that has only been a year at most. He's honestly the only person here she feels comfortable with.

Sean follows her gaze out the window. "Yeah, I think so. You'll need to ask Thomas, though. I think he was on the case, but I'm pretty sure Sarah said that it was just some punk teenagers looking to score enough for some fancy new sneakers that just released or something. Don't count on my word, though." He knew what his partner was thinking. Most likely something within the frames of, 'all those people out there are criminals and she just needs to figure out what they are doing.' He figures that's why their boss put them together. So he could keep Jane under control. He sees things differently. He's always been more of a trusting person. To him, they're just innocent people being targeted by the criminals and his job is to protect them all.

He watches Jane as she bites into her breakfast sandwich yet again, her straight black hair falling into her face. She blows at the strand, "Okay" is all she says.

Jane's phone buzzes on her hip. She reaches down and picks it up. "Jane here, what's up?"

Sean can hear a muffled reply and see a change in Jane's face. "We'll be there right away."

He raises an eyebrow at her, waiting patiently for her to tell him where they will be going. She puts her phone back on her hip and her eyes shift back, connecting with his. "Call about a murder. It's just down the street from here. They want us to investigate."

They pack up their breakfast as quickly as they can and head for the door, leaving the money and tip on the table. Jane glances back to make sure the waitress gets to it first. A blonde in a pink dress with a name tag reading "Kate" waves as she pockets the cash. Jane nods and follows her partner to the car, circling it and climbing into the driver's seat. Sean gets in on the passenger's side. Once inside the car, Jane flips the switches to turn on the siren and lights. She peels out and slings the car into traffic. As cars pull over to let her through, she speeds up, relaxing into a steady drive. Sean struggles next to her, trying to buckle and avoid spilling leftovers on himself. She tries to avoid being distracted by his fumbling. They are going so fast that by the time he finally settles in, Jane is putting on the blinker to pull into the driveway.

~~~~~

There are other detectives, including some county sheriff's already surveying the scene. Sean looks around the yard and notices a young woman crying. She's talking to a heavier set officer with orangish hair. Sean has seen him around the office but he's new, so his name always escapes him. The officer is taking the woman's statement, vigorously writing everything she says in a notebook.

Jane passes by him in a hurry. She's practically running and Sean huffs at the thought of trying to catch up to her. His partner is younger than he is and somehow seems to forget about that fact. He begrudgingly chases after her, anyway. They duck under the yellow caution tape and stroll inside the house. Jane walks up to the Sergeant on site. He's typing away on a tablet. "Hey Gregg, mind if we scan around at the scene?"

Gregg Sanders is a short, stocky man with gray hair and an unpleasant demeanor. He looks over his shoulder at her, annoyed by the interruption. "Yeah, to the left and then the second door on the right."

Sean takes the lead, and Jane follows behind. When they get to the room, it appears neat and everything seems in place. It would be hard to believe anything sinister went on in here... If it weren't for the man, around the age of 40, dangling from the ceiling, that is...

"It looks like he hung himself." Jane announces, deciding to state the obvious.

Sean gives her a sideways glance. Sometimes she just spouts off whatever pops into her head without fully analyzing things first. "Yeah, except, if you look, someone kissed him on his right cheek wearing some seriously bright red lipstick."

Jane walks to where Sean is standing and studies the man a little closer, mumbling out, "Sorry. I didn't see that before."

He glances over at her. "You've got to look at it from every angle, Jane." Sean puts on a pair of latex gloves and moves the man's head sideways a bit to look closer. "Think they can get a DNA sample off this?"

"I don't know." Jane puts on a pair of her own gloves and searches his arms for any other clues.

Just then Gregg saunters into the room. "We sent a sample off to see if we can. I highly doubt it, though."

"Yeah, that makes sense." Sean climbs up close and shines a light at the lipstick. "It looks pretty dry. We're not dealing with an amateur." He backs up to get a thorough look at the entire scene. "Just one question, though." He turns to look at Gregg. "Who could have done this, and why?"

Gregg just shrugs. "That's what we're working on now. It's obviously a female from the lipstick, but the question is, how did she get him up there?"

Sean nods his head in agreement.

Jane steps back now herself. "Maybe she has an accomplice."

Gregg gives a short bark of laughter. "Who would help her? What motive would they have? This kind of thing, the lipstick, just seems like a crime of passion or revenge to me."

Jane glares at Gregg and Sean notices the heat in her cheeks. If she's not careful, her attitude could really get her in trouble... He makes eye contact with her and gives her a warning look. Her shoulders relax a little as she turns back to Gregg. "Well... Maybe it was someone who hated this man just as much as she did. Besides, most killers who go to extremes like this normally have helpers. Right?"

She and Gregg go back and forth on the topic for a moment. Sean stands silently while they bicker about it. Finally, though, he steps forward and says, "Jane, I just don't think there was an accomplice. Looking around, I just don't see any signs of two people... if there were multiple people involved, they would have surely left behind some shred of evidence to suggest such... That being said though, I also don't think this was a woman. I think it had to be a male."

Gregg looks back at the body and cocks his head in confusion. "Why do you think that?"

"Well, first, this is giving me serious serial killer vibes and, by nature, they usually work alone. A female couldn't do all of this on her own. Women are typically physically weaker than men. The victim would have fought back, and he is obviously a fit man, so he would have overpowered a woman. Unless she was a bodybuilder or something... In addition, even if she drugged him or knocked him out, he would have then been dead weight. She wouldn't have been able to pick him up to hang him. So, all of that suggests that our killer is a male. He may have put fake lip marks on the cheek to throw us off track, and that would explain why the kiss mark was so dry. There was no saliva to wet it."

Jane nods at her partner. "I guess that makes sense."

"Well, I'll tell Dan what you said. That may lead us a little farther into this investigation." Gregg turns and walks out of the room. A few moments later, Sean notices him through the window walking across the yard towards Captain Dan Marshal, a tall sturdy man whose dark brown hair has some gray highlights streaking through at the top.

Jane lets out an inaudible sigh. "Every time I'm around that man, I get so angry." She glances over at her partner. "Did you see the way he just threw away my suggestion of an accomplice? Then you had to agree with him." She lets out a sigh.

Sean just ignores her and continues to examine the body. He's more interested in the crime than her bickering and complaining. Especially since this is such an interesting and unique crime compared to what they usually deal with.

Jane throws her arms up in the air and storms out of the room. He can hear her muttering, "I give up." as she strolls down the hallway.

He finally turns away and follows his partner out of the room. They search the rest of the house in silence. There is nothing else there. No fingerprints, no footprints, no hair left astray, or any piece of clothing caught on anything. Whoever did this had cleaned the house to perfection and nothing was out of place. It's a strange crime. Sean has to admit that much.

Later, they meet up at the police station to look things over and talk about the case. Captain Marshal, Sergeant Gregg, Jane, Sean, and a few of the other homicide detectives are there.

Gregg leans over and reviews the pictures they have laying out across the table. "So Captain, did you ever think about what I told you that Sean mentioned?"

Marshal nods. "Yeah, I did. It makes sense, but doesn't seem to fit."

Sean stares at Dan curiously. "Why not?"

"What would be the motive for him to kill another man, and why leave a kiss on his cheek in red lipstick?"

"Maybe he had quarrels with the man and used the kiss to throw us off? It wouldn't be the first time."

Marshal shook his head, "This isn't a normal murder, though. This kind often eventually turns into serial killings. They don't care about hiding their tracks, either. They want us to know who did it, and still not be able to catch them."

Sean thinks it over for a moment. "I guess you could be right."

Jane takes this opportunity to pipe up. "Then how would a woman be able to do all that by herself?"

Marshal sifts through the pictures again. "It's not the strangest thing to happen before."

Gregg peaks at the man's files. "Well, a year ago he cheated on his wife and she filed for divorce. The woman we saw at the scene was his girlfriend. The one he cheated on his wife with."

Sean scans through all the pictures lying on the table as well. He stops at one that shows the full scene of the man hanging from the ceiling. "A Judas killer." He mutters.

He had thought it was under his breath, but by the way everyone looks up at him; he realizes he was wrong. The heavy officer with the orange hair, whose name is apparently Sam, questions, "Excuse me?"

Sean peers back up at his companions. "A Judas killer. Judas betrayed Jesus with a kiss and was so ashamed he hung himself. This is like that. I think that's the connection." Sean smiles. "Many serial killers draw from old myths or religions. They aren't usually practicing... unless it's satanism... but they will often take something out of context from religion or mythology and use it as their theme or draw. This killer has apparently taken it upon their hands to find a betrayer and take matters into his or her hands to punish him for his crime. She, if the killer really is a she, believed he ought to be ashamed of himself and gave him the punishment Judas gave himself for his betrayal. Can we bring the ex-wife in for questioning?"

Marshal nods his agreement. "Yeah. I get what you're saying. I would have never thought of that." He looks around his group. "Sam, reach out to the ex-wife and have her come in for questioning. It wouldn't hurt to question the girlfriend some more, too. I hope this is just a revenge murder by the ex and not something more." He stared at the photos for a moment longer before finally blowing some air out between his lips. "Hm, a Judas Killer."

Chapter 2

She tapped her nail on the top of the desk rhythmically. *click. click. click.* Slow, methodical, matching the gears that turned in her mind as she stared at the instruments laid out in order before her.

The needles and small glass vials glimmered, catching the dim yellow light from her lamp placed at the edge of her desk as she checked, one last time, that all the components were present.

click. click. click.

She sat back, crossing her legs as she reached towards the bottom of the desk. Pulling open the clean white drawer, she gazed at the extra bottles neatly organized in rows.

Her voice was soft, just barely rumbling at the back of her throat, almost inaudible. "Hm." She balanced the bottle between the tips of her fingers as she held it up and inspected its contents.

"One more should do." She whispered out. She laid the vial out next to the others in the case. As she sat back once more in her seat.

click. click. click.

The thoughts churned in her mind once more, as she sat there for a moment longer before, finally, reaching towards the case and rolling it up, ready to be placed in her bag. Easing the case to the side, next to her lamp, she pulled out a file from the drawer on her other side.

The top flipped open to reveal pictures clipped to papers with neat cursive writing. Details of their lives and schedules of their days. Everything had been planned already and laid out perfectly.

Picking up the stack at the top, she inspected its contents. She removed the image of the man, with black salt and peppered hair groomed to the side. His grin was spread across his face, exposing perfect rows of white teeth, wrinkling the skin next to his dark eyes, showing off his age. She set it to the side and scanned the papers with his file. Forty-Six years old, had an ex-wife and lived with the former mistress.

She plucked the smooth metal pen from the container to her right and scratched away with the pen, writing out notes of the events that led up to his unfortunate demise. A smirk played at the edge of her lips as she thought about that night. Placing the pen down gently next to the file, she read over her smooth writing, making sure there were no errors. She would have to redo everything if there were.

Deciding all was right, she placed the papers and his image back together in the paper clip and added the newest image to the top. A stark contrast to the one beneath it, the dark, gritty, polaroid showed the same grayed hair and the shadow of wrinkles from the smile lines and stress of his life. In this one, however, his eyes were lidded and lifeless, and bright crimson lip marks stood out on his cheek, looking out of place and fake against his paling skin.

Perfect.

She opened a new file folder and laid his papers inside. The first of many to be added. She placed the new file in its proper drawer and leaned back, looking at the image and stack of papers that was once underneath his.

Click. Click. Click.

Chapter 3

The small meeting ends, and everyone meanders their way back to their respective departments. Jane and Sean shake hands with the others and go to leave when behind them they hear Captain Marshal's phone buzzing and he picks it up on the third ring.

"What?" the Captain exclaims. Jane turns toward Dan and watches as his face goes pale while he listens to whoever is on the other end of the phone. Marshal hangs up and studies Sean with narrowed eyes. Jane's partner fidgets uncomfortably before inquiring about the awkward stare down he's getting.

"Sean, it would seem that you are more than on the spot with your suggestions. Eerily so, in fact." Dan shakes his head and walks toward them. "Follow me." He leads them down the hall towards the elevator.

"Where are we heading?" Jane questions as she steps into the elevator, careful not to let it shut on her untied shoelace, kneeling to tie it once safely inside.

"Autopsy. There's something you ought to see." Dan scratches at the stubble on his face that was a couple days past due for a shaving.

"Can't you just tell us what it is? Is it really that important that we actually see it?"

"Well, from what I gathered from the phone call, yes, it is. You will most likely be interested in actually seeing it." He narrows his eyes at Sean again, who instinctively turns away. "And I'm just wondering how you knew so much."

"What do you mean, how did he know so much?" Jane asks, a bit annoyed by all the secrecy and the fact that it almost sounds like her partner is being accused of something. The elevator dings as they reach the lower level and exit. Captain Marshal marches on ahead of them, apparently avoiding explanation. It is only a short walk down the corridor to the autopsy room and they reach it in no time. Dan slides his key card through the slot and the door opens with a whir. A small man meets them just inside wearing gloves and a thin hospital robe over his clothes. His name is Jacob Roland, the county coroner.

"Hello, Captain. Jane. Sean. I think you're going to want to see this." He rushes over to a large metal table on the opposite side of the room. There is a dark olive green sheet covering a lumpy form that is undoubtedly the body of the victim. He pulls back the sheet to reveal the dark-haired man lying stiffly beneath.

"What is this all about, Jacob? We have already seen the body." Jane sighs stubbornly.

"Umm... well, this." He rolls the body over onto its stomach and Jane and Sean both gasp. On the man's back there, written in black sharpie the word "JUDAS". Jane shudders involuntarily and turns to face her partner.

~~~~~

Sean stares at the word with deep intensity but says nothing. The room is so quiet you could probably hear a feather hit the tile floor. Dan speaks, the first to break the silence.

"Sean, you were spot on. So how did you know?"

"I didn't." He glances up at the Captain, who's staring at him with concern, and reaches up to rub his face. "Don't look at me like that. It was just a lucky guess." He said.

"Lucky, yes. You should consider gambling. You would be rich." Dan says and narrows his eyes again.

"That's probably taking it a bit too far, don't you think..." Jane says defensively. She subconsciously steps between the Captain and her partner. Marshal doesn't notice but Sean does, and he raises an eyebrow briefly, considering what this gesture might imply. But he quickly forgets when his boss speaks again.

"I'm officially putting you both on the case. Effective immediately." He says and turns to leave, with Jane scrambling after him.

"Wait! You're putting us on the case? As in, without you? Doesn't the FBI usually handle the bigger cases like this? I don't think we are cut out for a serial killer case!"

Captain Marshal continues walking without turning back to face her. He is in charge and, frankly; it bothers him that the two detectives are questioning his judgment to begin with.

"Yes, I am. The FBI already knows about the case, but since it's not interstate, or serial murders yet, it's on us to solve. Besides, we don't know if it's going to become a serial or not. As of this moment, it's just a jealous ex-wife to me. On top of that, you seem to know a lot about it. Besides, I'm in charge and I'm assigning you two to this case, no ifs, and, or buts about it. Now get to work. You could start by revisiting the crime scene and looking for anything else we may have missed."

With that, Dan pushes the elevator button, and the door closes behind him. Sean turns back to thank Jacob before following Jane to the elevator. He's feeling nervous about the case and the word found on the victim's back. Even he can't deny how suspicious it looks that he knew about the Judas killer before they found the evidence of it. He had grown up in church and the case had simply struck a chord within his mind. It reminded him of the old stories he had read in the bible about Jesus and Judas and he had simply spoken it as it came. He doesn't speak his mind as much as Jane does, but he certainly can get himself into a bind when he chooses to...

Jane waits anxiously by the elevator with Sean lost in thought. It really ticked her off about being assigned to this case. A serial killer? Are they even ready for this? Is she? What is she talking about... Of course she is. If there's a madman, or in this case possibly mad women, out there somewhere, she would bring them to justice.

Sean scurries up beside her and they both file into the metal doors before them.

"So," Jane turns to her partner and gives him a curious gaze, "a lucky guess, huh?"

Sean shrugs, "It just rang a bell is all. I think Dan's suspicious of me, though."

"Well, yeah. I mean, that was crazy! You knew exactly what the killer was after. You can't help admitting that is really weird..."

"Yeah, but like I said, it was just a guess... How was I supposed to know? But at least it got us on the case. I mean, you seemed kind of upset, but I'm glad to---"

"I'm not upset!" She yelled.

"Sorry, I was just saying I'm glad we got it. If anyone can stop the killer, it's you."

Jane blushes but doesn't reply. The elevator door slides open and she hurries out.

Sean follows her quietly. He hadn't meant to make her feel awkward; she really is the best cop he knows. Aside from her occasional poor attitude. Jane ducks into the driver's seat of the black and white dodge charger. She's made mention several times how she can't understand how the station can afford such nice police cars when they are on such strict budgets these days. Sean climbs into the passenger seat next to her. He studies her carefully while she drives. He knows she is probably angry with herself for blushing earlier. She never blushes and she is always trying to hide her emotions from everyone.

Except anger, that is... She suddenly begins breathing faster, and he becomes somewhat concerned.

"You okay?" He asks.

"I'm fine!"

"Sounds like it." He says sarcastically, never taking his eyes off her.

She sighs and her breathing returns to normal.

"I'm okay, really. I want to be on the case, just wish he wouldn't be all high and mighty about it. He could have asked us first or something..."

"Yeah, I know what you mean. He is our boss, though." He points out the window ahead. "Hey, there it is. You can park there."

"I got it." She says.

They pull into the driveway and wave at the cops standing guard. Jane gets out and walks toward the yellow tape surrounding the house. Sean has to sprint to catch up with her and he lifts the tape for them both to go under. A few people on the street stop and stare at the house, but most of them have already gotten over their curiosity and moved on. They maneuver through the house silently, searching for any clue they may have missed the first time they surveyed the scene. Jane runs a finger along the top of a cabinet and it comes back clean. No dust.

"This place is spic and span. I mean like I could eat off of everything in here! Doubt we will find anything useful." Jane says.

"I agree. The killer knew what he, or rather she, was doing." John responds, looking around.

"So, do you want to head back, then? I mean, forensics looked this place over already, right?"

"Yeah, may as well. I doubt we do better than forensics did."

Jane takes one last look at the noose still hanging from the ceiling, and seeing nothing useful, turns to leave with Sean. She's thinking things over about the case and has a sudden thought.

"Do you think she'll have a schedule?" She asks.

"Who?" Sean looks confused as he turns back around to face her.

"The killer."

"What do you mean by schedule?"

"I mean, do you think she'll have a set time for her killings? When do you think she will strike again?" She responded.

"Jane, we don't even know if this is a serial killer case or not. As of this moment, we should treat this like any other homicide. She's probably just an angry mistress." Sane throws his hands up as if to say 'who knows'.

"Maybe... but I have a bad feeling about this case." Her eyes scan the room for a moment in concern.

"I know what you mean. I do too. But let's keep focus, we'll catch her. I know we will." He gives her a slight grin, trying to ease her worries.

"Well, I'm sure you're right. I just hope our feelings are wrong about this one, though."

They pile into the charger and drive off towards the station. Both have a lot on their minds and neither is looking forward to what may lie ahead...

Chapter 4

The young woman stared at the clear blue eyes of her next victim. It was hard to tell from the photo that he had blonde hair. It looked almost brown. He was younger than the last one, but that's okay. Age didn't matter, she would take care of all of them properly.

"Who was the poor lady who had to live with you?" She mumbled to herself as she looked underneath the photo. There in the notes, she saw her name, Vicky.

"I'm sorry you married such a filthy man, Vicky." She said, her voice cooed at the name on the paper. As she read on, she saw where Vicky was on a business trip this upcoming week. "Hm, that's perfect. I'll make sure he's never able to hurt you again, Vicky." She placed the paper down and looked at the photo again. Committing to memory who he was so she could spot him when the time was right.

Not like that was a problem. Everything was always perfect, never could go wrong.

She let out a squeak; the chair sliding out from under her as she stood abruptly. "What am I going to wear?" She placed the papers and image back together in the folder and shut it. She turned to leave, but stopped before reaching the door.

Going back to the desk with extreme care, she straightened the papers and folder, sliding them back into the drawer where she first retrieved them. It wouldn't do to make a mess of things.

No. Perfection. That's what was required.

After sorting out the papers and desk, she made her way towards her room, walking through the stark white of her home.

Perfection.

Everything, cleaned to a level of flawlessness you could only imagine in your dreams. That's the way it should be.

Everything was faultless, except the floors, that is. The white walls and furniture stood out against the darkness of the hardwood floors. They were out of place, had scratches and imperfections from age and use.

They would be the next to go.

With that thought in mind, she made her way up the stairs, checking the banister for dust. Of course there was none, but it didn't hurt to check. She would hate to make that mistake again.

No.

Not again.

Chapter 5

When Jane's phone rang around ten, she was already in bed. Seeing her partner's name light up on the screen gave her a mix of emotions. Another body already? Was there a break in the case? Or... what if it's not work related at all? Her face goes red, and she tries to push the thought aside. What on earth is wrong with her?

"Hello?"

"Uh, hey Jane... I was just... The case has me too stressed to sleep. I was wondering if you'd want to get a late drink and discuss it."

"Um," she sits up and glances down at her nightclothes. "Sure. Were you needing a ride?"

"Figured I'd cab there and back. Not sure how much I'll actually drink, but better safe than sorry."

"That's probably wise. I'll do the same. Meet you at Duke's in twenty ish?" She rolls out of bed and starts rifling through her dresser, holding the phone against her ear with her shoulder.

"Thanks." His voice sounds tired and groggy already... She's glad he's not driving.

"Of course. See ya soon."

~~~~~

Sean is already sitting at the bar with a whiskey glass in front of him when Jane walks in. He barely raises an eyebrow at her as she sits and flags down the bartender. She orders some fruity drink, and the guy behind the counter smirks. She pulls out her badge and places it on the bar in front of her, giving the grungy looking bartender a "I'm not in the mood look". His smirk drops and he nods in respect before turning to make the drink. Sean grins slightly. That's his partner.

He places the drink in front of her, and she takes a sip before turning to address him.

"So the whole Judas thing... How did you peg that so quickly?" She asks.

"You suspicious of me, too?" He groans and takes a small sip of his drink.

"No. Just curious... Are you religious or something?"

He stares at the glass in his hand. The harsh fluorescent lighting overhead reflected in the whiskey. He sets it down gently and pushes it slowly away from himself. Sighing.

"Probably not as much as I should be..."

"What exactly is that supposed to mean?" He senses some frustration in her question. As if she isn't even sure she cares, but felt compelled to ask, anyway. He shifts around on his stool uncomfortably.

"Nothing really. I just figured in our line of work it probably wouldn't hurt to have the big man on call more than just two days out of the year."

She gives him a confused look, and he rubs his face in exhaustion before attempting to explain further.

"I reckon if I only show up for him on Christmas and Easter, He won't show up for me the other 363 days of the year."

She's quiet for a moment, just swirling her straw around in her drink before she places a hand on his arm.

"I don't know a lot about God. I didn't grow up anywhere near religion. But I have a feeling that's probably not how it works..." she responds softly.

He glances up at her and they lock eyes. He can see authenticity in her eyes. Something genuine. Turning away again, he quickly pulls out his wallet. Sean lets a twenty fall to the counter before sliding off his bar stool.

"It's not... But it doesn't change the way I feel."

The bartender nods at them as they make their way out. Jane waves down a taxi and then turns back to her partner. She can tell this must really weigh on him. Honestly, she doesn't feel very qualified to discuss this with him. He needs a priest or something. But it hurts her to see her partner looking so lost.

"Well... If you feel that way, couldn't you just go back? If you think he shouldn't help you because you show up only twice a year, wouldn't it solve the issue if you just showed up more? Will he not accept you back?"

A street light above their head flickers and she watches his shoulders drop even further.

"He would... But I guess that's the other issue. I suppose I don't really feel worthy of being accepted..."

The taxi pulls up and Jane opens the door.

"Get in. You're drunk."

"You're funny." He frowns at her, and she puts her hands on her hips.

"Well, would you have admitted those feelings to me if you were sober?"

Sean looks at her, suddenly confused. As if he hadn't even realized that they'd been having a pretty personal conversation. She'd meant it more like a joke, but now she can't help but wonder. Maybe he really is drunk... How many glasses did he have before she got there? She can see his eyes cloud over as he considers her words. So she continues to express her thoughts about the matter.

"I doubt any human could live up to the standard of any God worth believing in. I mean, he'd be pretty pathetic if humanity, as crappy as it is, came close to being as good as him, right? After everything we see day to day? He better be way better than this mess for me to want to worship Him. So I'm gonna guess none of us would be worthy of acceptance. Yet as far as I can tell, there's a bunch of people who think He accepts them, anyway. What makes them better than you?"

He stares at her for a moment. The taxi driver growls at them to get in or shut the door. They climb in hastily. Jane gives the driver her address since she lives closest and then they sit in silence for a moment. Finally, after thinking it over a good long while, Sean responds to her question.

"You're right."

She raises an eyebrow. "I figured. But which part?"

"All of it. Thanks." he said.

He turns towards the window and stares out into the night. Neither speaks anymore. Jane gets out of the vehicle at her apartment and pays her share. She nods at Sean and he returns it before watching her disappear into the building.

"Where ya headin?" The taxi driver twists around to look at him.

Sean sighs, "Good question..."

Chapter 6

She stared at herself in the mirror of her room. Taking each delicate golden strand of hair and curl it to perfection. Any less would not be acceptable. She got up close to the mirror and with the utmost care, ran her coal black eyeliner around her shimmering green eyes. Only a little... too much and she would not look quite the way she needed to.

She added a few brushes of rouge on her cheeks. She didn't want to look pallid when she finally met her next victim. Then she reached down and, ever so gently and hesitantly, almost as if it were a sin, picked up the tube of deep red lipstick. While applying the lipstick, she smiled sweetly, her straight white teeth glistening in the pale light of the small fluorescent bulb above.

The woman walked to her bed and ran her hand over the silky emerald dress. She picked it up and slid it over her slip, smoothing it out. The bodice was tight fitting, so that she showed a good amount of cleavage and it clung tightly to her hips. The dress flared out towards the bottom but only a bit... Not like a mermaid style dress young girls wear to a prom or homecoming, but one with a simple, elegant flow about it.

She left her room and walked out the front door to the small yard hidden by a grove of acacia trees. She saw herself leaning against a midnight black Trans-am. The only difference between her and the reflection she was seeing was that the other had lips so blue they looked like the lips of a poor soul frozen in the coldest depths of the arctic.

Her reflection smiled sinfully at her. "Are you ready?" she asked.

She walked down the steps of the porch to stand in front of the other her. "Of course." She returned a smile, which to any onlooker would appear just as wicked as her reflections. She climbed into the car and dragged out into the night.

~~~~~

The blonde woman stepped out of the shadows of the alleyway, limping on a broken heel toward a man about to climb into his vehicle. He was a fine-looking young man, around thirty to forty years old. He had fair hair and blue eyes that looked like they could stare straight through you. It was him from the photo.

"Sir. Sir, please, can you help me?" She said it in her most desperate voice. She limped on towards the man, who had now paused halfway through the act of unlocking his car. "Sir, my fiancé and I got into an argument and he left me here. I have nowhere to go. And I broke my heel." She started crying. A trick she had mastered long ago. She knew her mascara ran down her face, but she didn't care. Crying would only help her right now.

The man's hand pulled back away from his car door, his key sliding out of the keyhole. "I-I'm sorry ma'am. What do you need from me? How can I help?" She could tell he had a hard time not letting his eyes drift down a few inches. Her amusement only grew inside and she had to fight herself not to allow a smile to form on her face as well.

"I need a place to stay for the night. I have no money and nowhere to go. I can't go home... Not with how my fiance is..." She gasped out her words as even more tears streamed down her face. She inched closer to the man, getting practically right up on him.

He couldn't help himself any longer. His eyes drifted down to her chest and his face flushed. "W-well. I guess I c-could help you." He struggled to lift his eyes up from the bodice of her dress with no luck.

She delicately pressed her hands onto his chest, batting her eyes at him like a lost puppy. "Really? Would you really help me?"

The man looked at her with pride in his eyes. "Yeah, my wife is on a business trip. You could stay at my place until you find somewhere else to go." He had finally pulled himself together to form a straight sentence without stammering.

She smiled up at him with those same big puppy dog eyes. "Oh, thank you! Thank you so much!"

She limped to the passenger's side of the car. The man followed her and unlocked the door to let her in.

Chapter 7

Sean wakes up at three in the morning to his phone going off. He reaches over to the nightstand and picks it up, fumbling to get a good grip on it as his eyes adjust.

"Hello?" His voice, still groggy from sleep, came out hoarse, causing him to clear his throat.

"Sean, we need you now, downtown. There's been another murder." Sean instantly recognizes Captain Marshall's voice.

He sits up in bed and rubs the sleep out of his eyes with his free hand. There's only a slight throbbing in his temple. It could be from earlier in the night or possibly just the lack of sleep. He's glad he didn't drink more than a glass or two. Although his partner probably thinks he drank more than that after some of his reactions to the conversation.

"I'll be there in a sec." He announces into the phone speaker before hanging up.

He climbs out of bed and rushes around the room, quickly throwing on his bulletproof vest and some boots that could really use a good washing. Grabbing his keys on his way out the front door, he runs down the stairs of his front porch to his small Ford Focus that's parked out front. Jumping into it, he speeds out of the driveway and onto the road in front of his house. He's yawning constantly and smacks his face a few times, trying to wake up. With the empty roads stretched out before him, he speeds up and reaches over to hit the button on his CB. "Sean here. Can you give me the location again?"

The rooky, Sam, replies with the address of the house and a few descriptive details.

Sean drives for about twenty minutes before he pulls into the gravel covered ground in front of the house. There are police vehicles all along the road and despite the late hour, there is still a good crowd of pedestrians trying to get as close as possible. Of course, the lights and sirens would attract at least the neighbors, probably. Some people just can't help but be nosy. Although he doesn't blame them, often he's nosy from afar, too.

Sean climbs out of his vehicle and races to where Jane is standing up ahead. She looks over at him, glances away, and then quickly jerks her head back around.

Her eyes get wide and her face turns beat red before she finally busts out laughing. "Sean, I know they said to hurry, but you could have at least put on some decent clothes!"

He looks down at himself and moans. He has his vest on... but below he's wearing nothing but a white undershirt and his boxers with rubber ducks all over them.

"Sorry. I just woke up and ran out the door..." Heat rushes to his face, but he tries to play it off.

Jane looks down at his boots. "Fancy yourself a cowboy, huh?"

Sean gives her the death glare. But then it could be worse... You would think if she was going to make fun of something it would be his boxers or something from their conversation last night... Actually, she's probably toning down the mocking because of their conversation at the bar. "Does it matter?" he mumbles, avoiding eye contact.

~~~~~

Jane is having a hard time trying to keep from laughing. Sean is standing in front of her in a pajama shirt, ducky boxers, and some boots that are obviously covered in something other than mud. And she doesn't even want to know what. "No. No, it doesn't matter at all." She doesn't mind the tight fitting night clothes, anyway. He takes good care of his body and it shows. Especially now. In fact, it tempted her to whistle when he first showed up. But they don't really have that kind of relationship yet... and after a few hours ago... That probably would have been really awkward.

But his lack of clothes is still amusing none-the-less.

Of course, the boss probably won't be thrilled... Her partner better hope Captain Marshall is in a good mood this morning or he might just chap his hide for this. She giggles a bit at the connection between her thoughts and her partner's boots. He gives her another look, obviously attributing her giggles to more teasing. Oops...

~~~~~

Sean walks on by his mocking partner and into the house. He finds Dan standing in front of a fair-haired man who, like the other man, is hanging in the middle of his bedroom.

Marshall looks over at Sean and smiles a bit. "I remember the first time they put me in charge of a killer's case. I couldn't remember if I had put my pants on or not either, but I eventually remembered before I left the house…"

Sean doesn't even look at him. He just growls, "Oh shut up. It's 3:00 a.m."

Although it's no doubt hard to stay serious, Dan manages to for a moment. "You know why I put you on this investigation, right?"

Sean closes his eyes and sighs.

"No, I don't. I think it may have been a pretty wrong choice, though, considering what I'm wearing… And what happened last time."

Dan smiles softly at the young man standing in front of him. He is in his early thirties, graduated law school early, joined the force, climbed the ladder up to head investigator, and being so young, made a mistake and they demoted him back to a regular detective to work with those his age whom he should have graduated with. "That's exactly why I put you on this investigation. You may have made a mistake in the past, but you are cunning and perceptive. There was a reason you were the top investigator within a year, even if you were the youngest. Somehow, you know how the killers think. Don't ask me why and I'm also a little worried why, but you do. So for now I'm promoting you to head investigator, only for this case, though it could be permanent if you play your cards right."

Sean just stares at the detective. He isn't sure this man is making the right decision. He's okay with the position he is in now. People still come to him for his input on things, but he doesn't get the problem of having to take the blame if things go wrong. "What about Jane?" he asked.

"She can tag along. Besides, I think you need her to protect you. She's got promise and you're not so good at doing that on your own, anyway." They both grin, as if sharing an inside joke. A distant memory from when Sean was still the head investigator flashes to mind.

"Alright, but if things go wrong, it's on your head this time, not mine. Let it be known that I think you're making a mistake." Sean stated.

"Duly noted." Dan pats Sean on the back before both men survey the room. The man hanging from the ceiling this time has the red kiss on his right cheek just like the last. And upon lifting his shirt, they find "JUDAS" written in black sharpie across his back, same as the previous victim.

This house, just like the last, is spotless. There is no sign of dust anywhere in the house. No footprints, fingerprints, or anything else left behind, not that they can find, anyway.

Sean glances over at Dan. "So this *is* turning out to be more than just a vengeful ex, huh? This is gonna be a hard case to crack."

Captain Marshall nods his agreement. "Seems that way you better get on it."

"Of course. Right away, sir." Sean responds.

"And Sean..."

"Yes, sir?" he asks.

"Put some pants on first."

"Yes, sir."

Chapter 8

The beautiful young woman twirled in her long, flowing dress. It was a fiery orange color with gold and red stitching. Her curls bounced around her head and she giggled absent mindedly.

"Don't I look gorgeous?" She grinned at the other her who nodded solemnly.

"It's time, huh?" Again, her reflection nodded.

"Okay, here goes." She turned to the door and walked out and down the stairs.

The girl moved about the inside of the bar, searching for her next victim. A tall man with dark hair sat at the bar, practically drowning in some cheap whiskey. She moved over and sat next to him, eying the ring on his finger. This is the one. Show time, she thinks as she leans in close to him.

"Hey there, cutie, whatcha drinking?"

He turned and gave her a besotted smirk. She could see he was gone, wasted, and he was looking her over with lustful intensity.

"I was drinking whiskey, but now I'm drinking in your beauty."

It was kind of corny, but what did she expect from a drunkard?

"Oh, really?" She whispered in his ear before teasing him and turning away.

"Let me buy you a drink?"

"Sure, but that's not really what I want..."

His grin spread across his face, and his eyes shone. He was falling right into her hands. The man cleared his throat and asked for the check. Looking at it, he threw down a few bills and stood up. She grabbed his hand and led him toward the door, giggling as they moved through the mass of bodies.

"My roommate's home and she won't be happy if I bring you there..." she mumbled the words out, seeming unsure of how he would react. "Do you have a place we could go?" She put on her most sincere pouty face and he grinned devilishly.

"Yeah, I may have a place." He answered.

"Great!"

He lifted his leg over a black Harley Davidson with chrome wheels and turned around to nod at her. She slowly slid her leg over behind him and wrapped her arms around his waist. She giggled as he sped down the street, everything was going just as she had planned it. They pulled up to a small log cabin in the woods nearby. It was a cute little cabin. A simple front porch with a couple of windows looked as though the inside only had a couple of rooms.

"This is where I stay when I go hunting. Nobody will bother us here." He told her.

"It's perfect."

A grin spread across her face as he led her into the cabin. She paused in the doorway and turned to glance at the other her, unfurling from behind a tree. The man felt her stop and turned to look back at her. He saw her staring out the door and looked over her shoulder at an empty yard.

"Whatcha looking at, gorgeous? Having second thoughts?" He asked.

She flipped her hair over her shoulder as she twisted back around to see him. Her smile gleamed in the moonlight, and she grabbed his hand and pulled him farther inside.

"No. Not one." She said.

Chapter 9

Jane's alarm rings at four am. An early bird, as always, she sits up and hits the off button for the alarm on the clock/radio. Her bathroom is only a few yards away on the other side of her bedroom and she makes her way there swiftly. Her sweat soaked the dark gray tank top she wore to sleep, and she knows she needs a shower. Flipping on the shower head she strips and climbs in, taking her time to soak up the hot water and relax for a moment.

Once out, she dries her hair with a towel and brushes it through before depositing it into a thin black ponytail. The coffee pot on the stove clicks to alert her it's ready and she saunters over to pour a cup. She has just taken a sip as she hears her phone vibrate on the counter and she reaches over, lifting it up enough to read the words on the screen as she takes another sip of her coffee. It's a text from Captain Marshall and it's not good.

~~~~~

Sean groans as his phone buzzes on the table nearby. He reaches for it, noticing that it's Jane calling, and flips it open.

"Mmm Hmm....?"

"You up?" She asks.

"I am now."

"Well, good. Judas struck again."

"Again?!" He bolted upright in bed.

"Yes, again. At least we have a timeline now. It seems as though she's killing them around every three days." She responds.

"Is that a good thing? That's not long between victims."

"Good? Well, I mean, we know when to expect them. But no, it doesn't give us much time to do anything about it. It does, however, tell us they are not pre-selected. Most likely, anyway. She is probably choosing victims that meet her criteria at random. I mean, that's what would make the most sense to me, anyway. Just get there as soon as you can, okay?"

"On my way." he groans again and clicks the phone shut. Rolling out of bed.

~~~~~

Plants and trees surround the crime scene. The cabin lies ahead and Jane arrives late, cause being a very frustrating old lady that refused to leave her alone. Something about a cat in a tree or something of the sort. She didn't have time for that, so she had given the lady the number for the fire department and moved on to the crime scene.

She finds her way along the brush towards Sean upon arrival. He laughs as she steps over animal scat and other outdoor remnants that he can tell is totally grossing her out. She's definitely a city girl. No wonder she mocked his boots.

"If I remember correctly, you called me this morning, telling *me* to meet *you* here." He shakes his head at her.

"Oh, shut up." She hisses.

"What kept you?"

"A very persistent old woman with a cat up a tree." She replies.

"That's hilarious. I mean kind of cliche. I'm almost inclined to not believe you." He's looks down at her, humor in his eyes.

She sticks out her tongue like a 5-year-old at him. "Just show me the scene. Although I imagine it looks the same as all the others?"

"It does. Right this way."

They stroll through the doorway of the cabin. The interior is calming, complete with a sizzling fireplace and leather sofa that's placed around a medium-sized brown coffee table resting in the center of the room. Jane follows Sean to a room on the left that is so grand that it had to be the main bedroom. It has cranberry curtains and a large canopy bed. The room is in perfect balance... besides the dead body draping from the ceiling, of course. As with the last victims, there is no blood, only a red kiss on the cheek and Judas written on the back. Jane circles the man and then looks back at Sean.

"Have we learned anything new from Autopsy yet?"

"Yes, looks like they used drugs before hanging them up," He nods solemnly.

"With what?" She turns back to the body, eyes squinting as though she can find all the answers there if she just looks hard enough.

"Quetiapine."

"What kind of drug is that?" She asks. Her eyebrows raise in curiosity.

"It's an antipsychotic. It's sometimes used as a tranquilizer and is most commonly used to treat schizophrenia."

"So our killer is a schizophrenic? I could have told you that much!" She gestures at the dead body as if to say 'here's proof'.

"Probably, but I highly doubt she's taking the meds herself." Sean lifts his hand to his chin as he thinks it over.

"Okay, well, wouldn't she need a prescription to get her hands on those drugs? Why don't we check with all the nearby hospitals to see who all is on this drug right now?"

"That's probably the best idea you've ever had." Sean smiles at her. It was supposed to be a compliment, but it came out sarcastic. Instead of trying to correct his tone, he decides that it's probably for the best and leaves it at that. To be honest, if it had come out the way he meant it in his head, she might have gotten the wrong idea, anyway...

"Thanks. Now let's go, smart alec."

Sean lets out a small laugh to hide the fact that his 'smart alec response' wasn't taken as intended before trailing after her. At least they have a lead now. This case is ridiculous. A victim every three days? That's a lot of victims in a short time frame. They are going to have to be on the ball with this one or they could end up in a panic throughout the state. Things are already heating up as the news media has finally gotten some information about the first two murders.

But the killer is working faster than they are; Sean has never seen a serial killer claim victims in such short periods of time. At least not in his area before... He can only hope the killer will move so fast that she will make a mistake. And if she does, he and Jane will be there to find it.

~~~~~

Her partner is poring over all the pictures hanging on the wall of his office when Jane strolls in.

"Hey, Sean."

"Hey." He has one hand resting lightly on his mouth and chin, muffling his voice when he talks. "Just looking over everything." He explains.

Jane leans against Sean's desk and crosses her arms, following his gaze to the wall. "Yeah, I've been doing that all day, too. There is really nothing else to do. We could go look at the crime scene again, but it will be the same. Cleaned to perfection." Her words sound hopeless, but her tone says otherwise...

Sean drops his hand and looks over at her. "You have an idea, don't you?"

Jane just nods, but goes back to staring at the pictures without continuing.

"Well, what is it?" Sean's curiosity is building, and he turns his body to her, obviously trying to show he's genuinely interested.

He's so close Jane has to look up to make eye contact. "The killer has been going after married men who have cheated on their wives, right?"

Sean mumbles in agreement and she continues, "Then why don't we have one go in as a spy? Report what she looks like, if she mentions any place that she may take him... It's a long shot, but it's the only thing I think we can do at this point."

He considers it a moment before mentioning, "The problem is knowing exactly when and where she is going to strike next."

"Yeah. That's why I have been studying her route." Jane walks to the other side of Sean's desk and looks at the map he has laid out. "Looks like you've been doing the same."

"Yeah, I've been wondering if there's a pattern so that we can tell where she'll strike next." Sean strolls over to Jane and leans down to study over her shoulder.

Jane can feel him brushing against her back. She feels heat creep up her face and is glad he can't see her right now.

He points at a spot on the map. "This is where the first murder was. I asked around, and almost all the people said they saw him at the casino downtown the night before. I'm guessing that's where she found him. His girlfriend was out-of-town visiting a friend and got home that morning. The next murder was also at the man's home." Sean moves his finger to another spot down one row of streets and three houses away from the last.

"The last place they saw him was at the grocery store. No help there, but his wife was also out of town that day. And our most recent murder was at the man's hunting cabin." Sean slides his finger to a place out in the woods. "But his home was here." He moves his finger to a spot on the map down a row of streets and three houses down from the last. "His wife was also out, but he had a teenage son at home. The last place they saw him was at a bar. So my question is, how has our murderer known when someone was at the house, and when someone was not? Also, how did she know that man owned a cabin in the woods?"

Jane stared at the map. "Do you not see the pattern? It's obvious our killer is going to strike here." She pointed at a spot down a row of streets and three houses away from the last.

"There's a problem with that one, though. He doesn't cheat on his wife, because he isn't and has never been married or in a committed relationship. I've already looked into him."

Jane removed her finger. "Oh. Then how do we know where she'll strike next?"

"I'm not sure, but if we can figure out how she knows all of this, then maybe we'll figure that out." Sean leans back from the map and glances over at the pictures again. "There's just something off about these murders that I can't quite figure out."

"Do you think the murderer doesn't know any of this? That she is trusting the men to know?" Jane asks, glancing at him.

Sean gives Jane a puzzled look. "What do you mean?"

"Maybe she met those men at the last places they were seen, and they took her to where they would be alone. As in, she is seducing the men, knowing they'll follow along because they cheat on their wives all the time."

"I didn't think about that." Jane watches Sean's expression change to one of realization. "The cameras at the grocery store and casino... if you're right, Jane, they would have recorded the whole thing!"

Jane stands up and runs out the door. Sean follows, hot on her heels. They hurry past other offices and the people inside give them dirty looks for the noise. When they get to the elevator, Jane pushes the down button impatiently. "Wish this stupid thing would hurry." She grumbles, turning to Sean. "Do you think this is it? I mean, really it?" Her excitement was present in her tone.

"There's only one way to know..." The elevator doors open and the two rush inside. Sean pushes the first floor button and the doors close. The mechanisms above them whir as they work to lower the elevator to the first floor. He's slightly annoyed at the flickering light above his head, but there is no time to worry about changing a bulb right now. He will let the maintenance man know about it eventually, though.

They march through the front doors of the building. Jane strides around the hood of the car and hops in the driver's seat as Sean climbs in the passenger's.

It's only moments later that they pull up to the grocery store. The two of them climb out of the vehicle and walk through the lone sliding door at the front of the building. Sean hears the bell jingle above his head, alerting the staff that a new customer has arrived. Jane moves to the front checkouts and asks the closest cashier a question, most likely where the manager is. Sean looks around the aisles as he slowly heads over to them. Once he refocuses his attention ahead, he notices the cashier has now disappeared.

Jane glances over her shoulder at him. "He went to get the tapes for that night from his manager."

"Good. I hope we are right about this, Jane. This would be our first big break-through." The cashier comes back with a box in his hand.

"Here. These are all the tapes from six in the afternoon to six in the morning on the day you mentioned."

Jane takes the box from him and nods appreciatively. "Thank you."

They slink back to the car and climb inside. Jane sets the box in Sean's lap. "Here, you can hold this while I drive." She asserts. He doesn't complain.

~~~~~

Back in his office, Sean sits down in the large black rolling chair at his desk. Jane slides one of the tapes into the VCR and turns it on. They speed the video up, but there is nothing suspicious. So they do the same with the next two tapes, and finally, on the fourth tape, they notice something. Sean backs it up and slows it down as the two move closer to the screen.

A girl, in her mid-twenties It would seem, walks towards a car with a man about to get inside. Upon looking closer, Sean realizes it's one of their murder victims.

"This is it!" They watch and realize the girl, as Jane had said, appears to be seducing the man. She is also limping in the video. "Do you think she's crippled?" Sean asks, confused. A single female subduing and killing these men is crazy enough, but a crippled one?

Jane gives Sean a look. "No genius. She has a broken heel."

"Well, sorry... I didn't notice that from this far away..."

The girl in the video walks around to the passenger's side, and the man lets her in.

"Well... That's that I guess. We still can't see what she looks like for sure from this angle, but at least we know how she does what she does. It looks like she may have light colored hair, though. The black and white film makes it hard to tell, but I would definitely say there's a good chance she's blonde." Jane stands up and takes the tape out of the VCR. She puts it on Sean's desk. "Might want to show that to Dan. He may find it interesting."

"Alright." Sean nods and Jane leaves him alone in his office to contemplate things. Finally, he gets up and goes to show the tape to Captain Marshall to see what he thinks.

Chapter 10

"Don't look at me like that!" The girl slipped the midnight blue dress over her head as she complained to the other her. The dress came down only a few inches past her waist and hugged her hips securely. The other her watched with a disapproving look as she put on her blood red lipstick and adjusted her hat. She finished and turned to her reflection. She held her arms out to the side as if to ask, 'What do you think?' The other her answered the unspoken question with one of her own.

"You're going to the races in that hat?"

"Yes, I am. All ladies wear enormous hats at the racetrack." She answered.

"In what century?"

"This one! Now, if you're quite finished, it is time to go."

She left the room and made her way outside. She met the taxi down the street. No sense giving out their address and risking someone finding them. Then at the track, she paid her way in with cash. The other her has always been against having bank accounts and cards tied to her name. Inside, people were bustling all around to place bets.

Large televisions in each corner showed the odds of each horse. What most people don't seem to realize, though, is that those odds are the odds that a horse will lose, not that it will win. So if a horse's odds are 3:1, then he is most likely to lose. This is how the track makes money; they trick the people into betting on the wrong horse. She admires the track for this; it is very deceptive, just like her. She never had seen herself admiring the quality of deceit... The other her, however...

At the tiller nearby, a man pulls out a stack of hundreds and hands it over. He glanced over his shoulder anxiously and spotted her. He winked at her and she rolled her eyes. Immediately, his face fell, and he turned back to the window, ego wounded. It's apparent he's a sleazeball, but he isn't her mark. A sign nearby pointed to a room just off to her left and she made her way toward it. She handed the large man guarding the door a sizable sum of cash, and he stepped aside to let her through, no questions asked.

Inside the room, there was a large poker table surrounded by six men and one woman, who could only be the dealer. The men turned as she entered and glared at her, frustrated at having their game interrupted. Some men gave her angry looks and others seemed to flirt with her, but either way, she didn't care.

She watched them play and studied each one. She's pretty good at reading people. If she ever had the opportunity, she thinks she would enjoy playing poker herself. Maybe she could win a decent amount of money for herself. And the other her, of course...

One man, a burly fellow named Rick Steele, was a terrible gambler and had already lost almost everything he had. He had an easy to spot tell, which is probably the reason he was losing so badly. Another guy, known only by ACE, must be a pro or a cheater, from the size of his winnings so far. Probably the latter, considering the dealer, kept winking at him when the other men weren't watching. However, the man she was most interested in was called Straight. He was a slender man with dark spiked hair and a gold wedding ring around his finger. His real name was Less Walters, which she only knew because noted in her information. He wasn't losing as bad as Rick but he also wasn't doing good like ACE, however he was holding his own.

When the game was over, ACE had won and sauntered off to cash in his chips. Several of the men cursed as they packed up their stuff and one man actually broke into tears, having lost everything. Less gathered his remaining chips up quietly and tipped his hat to the dealer before turning to leave. The girl met him in the doorway and he seemed to notice her for the first time since she had arrived.

"You did really well in there." She said, smiling coolly.

"Well, thank you, would have done even better if that good for nothing ACE hadn't had the dealer in his pocket."

"Yeah, I noticed that."

"You did? Well, you're beautiful and smart then. A lot smarter than some of these idiots around here, that's for sure!" He responded.

"Thanks, you're so sweet."

"My pleasure. So, do you always go to the races to watch men play poker?"

"No, sometimes I go to watch them play pool." She teased.

"Ha, funny. Alright, you can call me Less. And what may I call you?" He asked.

"That depends on how well you plan to get to know me."

"Wow, am I sensing a little something behind that?"

"Maybe... I am a fairly forward person. Call me Lucy." She said.

"I see, well in that case, Lucy, I would like to get to know you very well."

Chapter 11

Sean dashes into Jane's office at top speed. When he arrives, he is so out of breath that he can't even talk. All he can do is lean against the door frame, panting. Jane watches the panting Sean with mild interest. Poor guy had recently put on a few pounds and, although he still has a gorgeous figure, he could use some more exercise to avoid things like this. She thinks the case is getting to him so much he hasn't been keeping track of his health as much as he usually does.

"Let me guess," she sighs. "Judas struck again?"

He nods, still wheezing. Jane shakes her head and grabs her keys. Sean, finally catching his breath, gives her the address and they head out. As usual, Jane does the driving and doesn't really give her partner a say in the matter. Hotel staff found the body in a room that the victim had signed and paid for. As always, the room is completely clean and there are no signs of a struggle. The victim has a red kiss on his right cheek and "Judas" on his back, as always. Jane looks the body over and turns to her partner.

"Did anything ever come back about that drug?" She asks.

"You mean the antipsychotic tranquilizer?"

"Yeah, the one the killer uses to sedate the victims." She circles the body again.

"Dan's been checking into it, but there's the whole doctor patient confidentiality thing." Sean responds.

"Yeah, well, there is also the whole serial killer on the loose thing! That should trump doctor patient confidentiality!" Her voice rises in frustration.

"It should, but it doesn't. At least not without a court order..."

"That's so stupid!" She turns abruptly to face him.

"Well, like I said, Dan's working on it. He's talking to the DA. I'm sure he will find a way around it soon."

"I hope so."

Jane takes one more look around the room and sighs.

"There's nothing to do here. As always. Why don't we go check out the video cameras at the racetrack? The hotel manager said the guy mentioned something about having just come from the races."

"Did the clerk see the woman? What did the cameras here show? Did we even ask for the footage?" Sean rubs his chin thoughtfully.

"The clerk said the victim is the only one who came in. And he didn't mention having a second guest with him. Unfortunately, the hotel's cameras are apparently just for looks. We gave the owner a citation and told him to invest in real cameras. But there's nothing more to do here. The track should have some actual footage." Jane steps aside as the coroner and crew make their way into the room.

"Yeah, I guess that's the best thing we can do for now. Hopefully, they will have better footage than the grocery store. Besides, forensics needs this room, so we should get out of their way." Sean nods and the two head out.

~~~~~

Sean calls the racetrack and has them tell the manager to get the tapes ready for them. Jane drives while Sean is on the phone with Captain Marshall, explaining what they intend to do.

When they arrive at the track, the manager meets them at the front door and hands them the box of tapes.

"These are all the tapes from last night." The short, gravelly sounding man seems irritated that their investigation has interrupted his business.

Sean takes the box from his hands and excuses him back to his work. There are a lot of tapes to go through and Sean groans, thinking about how long it'll likely take to look through all of them. He shuffles back to the car while glancing over at the horses and their trainers in the tracks. It's been a while since he's been to the races. Maybe if things ever slow down and this case ever wraps up, he'll take the time to go again. He's never really been a betting man, though. He really just enjoys watching the horses run.

Jane opens the back door for him and he sets the box in the seat with a thud. He straightens up and pops his back a bit with a small moan.

Jane chuckles. "Getting out of shape, are you?"

Sean shakes his head, his face turns a slight shade of pink. "No, I just haven't had time to work out this past month..."

"Oh, so you work out?" Jane wiggles her eyebrows at him playfully.

But Sean seems dead serious when he responds, "Yeah. What did you think I did in my free time?"

Jane can't hold it in anymore and bursts out laughing. "Sean, you crack me up." But she can immediately see that he's utterly confused by the situation, so she stops and shakes her head. "Never mind. Get in the car and let's go get started on the tapes."

Somehow, everything goes over his head. He's just so literal sometimes...

Jane drives them back to HQ, singing along with the radio the entire time. Sean can't help but think she must be tone deaf. The longer it goes on, the more he really wants her to shut up, but he holds his tongue, trying to let her have her fun since she's in an unusually good mood today.

When they arrive back at HQ, they take the elevator up to Sean's office. The light is still not working. He can't remember if he ever told anyone about it or not... He unlocks the door to his office for them and gets the TV and VCR ready while Jane sorts through the tapes.

Sean plops down in his chair and Jane takes a spot on the floor, leaning back against the back wall, and making herself as comfortable as possible. The first tape they put in shows a video of some men playing poker and the dealer walking around the table. There is also another woman in the room standing in a corner watching the game progress. Her enormous hat hides most of her face from view.

When the game ends, the woman approaches a man that was sitting at the table. They leave the room together after talking for just a few brief moments.

Jane stops the tape and whips her head to face Sean. "Was that our man?" She asks excitedly.

"I think so. Rewind it a bit." Sean leans forward in concentration.

Jane rewinds it, but they still can't get a clear image of the man in the video. However, after discussing it and playing it back several times, they decide they are pretty sure that this is the victim. He looks like the same body type. But despite the off angle of the victim, the good part is they get a pretty clear view of the woman. The film is in black and white, but she is close enough to the camera for them to notice she's wearing dark lipstick, most likely the deep red they are looking for. This video is even clearer than the grocery store video. And you can definitely tell her hair must be blonde in this one. It's such a light gray color on the video there's no denying it. And even though they can't see her face clearly because of the hat, the rest of her slender yet elegant features show clearly.

Jane figures if she were to see this woman on the street, recognizing her should be pretty easy just by what they can see.

Chapter 12

She was lying in her bed staring at the other her. "Do you think they'll catch us?"

The other her laughed. "No. They're not that smart. Besides, we've been leading them in circles. So no, they won't catch us."

"When do we get dad?"

Her reflection was spinning in a computer chair and stopped. She looked over at the girl lying in the bed. "When I say so."

The girl on the bed nodded her head as if this answer was acceptable. "Okay, so who's next?"

Her other stood up and walked over to the desk. She read from the piece of paper that was placed on top. "He's thirty-five years old, and has cheated on his wife. Multiple occasions."

"That piece of scum! Several times? How can men be like that?" The girl responded, jerking up to look.

The other her glared at her in frustration. "Please don't interrupt me, Shanna. His name is Richard Williams, but his friends call him Rick. He'll be at a football game this Saturday, three days away. I have a dress picked out for you already, and I want you to go try it on." She set the piece of paper down. "It's upstairs in my closet. The green one."

"Ooh, I like the color green. Does it match my eyes?" Shanna batted her eyelashes at her reflection.

"Yes, I made sure of that. The blue one the other day clashed. Now go try it on."

"Okay." Shanna jumped out of bed and raced up the carpeted stairs to the other hers bedroom. She opened the door and looked around. Everything in the room was pure white, and you would never find a speck of dust because she always cleaned it to perfection. It was almost as if nobody lived in the room at all, but of course that would be ridiculous because the other her lived there…

She opened up the closet, and there was a green dress hanging on the inside of the door. She took it down and laid it on the bed, marveling at all the different shades of green that ran through it. It had a heart-shaped neckline and it would fall loosely to her knees.

Shanna stripped out of her nightgown and pulled the dress over her head. She turned to the full body mirror on the wall beside her reflection's dresser and looked at herself. The dress fit her perfectly. It didn't hug too tight, but it showed off all of her curves modestly. It wasn't what she was used to, but she had to trust the other her or things wouldn't go as planned.

She saw the other her in the mirror and smiled. "It's beautiful, I love it."

Her reflection smiled back. "Good. I have some shoes that would go great with that."

Shanna twisted around in the dress and watched the shimmering green silk change shades. Like she said, it matched her eyes and made them look even brighter than they really were.

Chapter 13

"I understand. Thanks for the call." Sean hangs up his phone and looks solemnly up at Jane. He has just gotten off the phone with Captain Marshall and has some rather bad news to tell his partner.

"Bad news."

"I can tell by your face. Spill." Jane raises an eyebrow.

"Dan got the names of all the people prescribed Quetiapine in the last three years." He responds.

"Okay, how is that a bad thing?"

"Our killer isn't there."

"How do they know?" She asks, bewildered.

"They checked everyone on the list. They are all either really old, male, in prison, in a nuthouse, or dead."

"Well, that's just great. Back to square one, I suppose." She kicks at the floor.

"Not exactly. We still have a chance. She has to get the drug somewhere, right?"

The way Sean's face looks as he asks that question tells Jane exactly what he has in mind.

"You're thinking black market, aren't you?" Her eyebrows raise as she gives him a look.

"It's worth a shot. There are only two dealers I know of near here. It could be worth it to show the girl's photo to them." Sean shrugs as if what he's suggesting is nothing.

"I doubt a black market dealer is going to give up a buyer to the cops." She shakes her head, "if you catch my drift... They will tuck tail and run the second they see us coming."

"That's why we go undercover. We pretend we're there to buy. It gets us in and we can threaten them with arrest or something. We can make them a deal. We will let them off easy if they give us a name and address." He responds, giving a curt shrug of his shoulders.

"I still don't think it's going to work." Her face scrunches up as she thinks it over.

"It will, has to. It's the only thing we've got to go on right now."

Just then, Jane's phone chirps and the screen lights up with a text message. She reads it and shakes her head.

"That's not the only thing we have. Apparently, we have fingerprints."

Sean's eyes go wide. Could the killer really have been so careless? He just can't see their Judas making such a drastic mistake...

"You're kidding." He rubs at his chin.

"No actually, I'm not. They found them on the bottom of the last victim's shoe. Probably from when the killer was lifting him." She says.

"That's...... great." He mutters, looking off in thought.

"Not that it helps us much."

"What do you mean?" He comes out of his trance, eyebrows drawing together.

"I mean, she isn't in the system. There are no matches showing up on the computer for her prints. At least no exact matches. They are looking into something but didn't say what."

"Well, at least now if we bring someone in, we can compare their prints to those." He responds.

"Yeah, I guess there is that." She nods.

"Well, let's get going. First stop, Ricardo Bonanno of the downtown mafia." Sean grabs his phone off his desk and holds his arm out towards the door as if to let Jane go first.

"Great... We are going to die." She mutters as she brushes past him, sighing.

Sean chuckles and follows her out. He flips the light off behind him and closes the door.

Ricardo, who goes by Lil Ric most of the time, is the leader of the East New York Mafia, or ENYM for short. He has a well-known reputation as a ruthless criminal, but somehow he always escapes the law. Evidence just goes missing... You know?

Back when Sean was the head investigator, he had gotten himself in a bind with the ENYM. Lil Ric was second in command then. The leader at the time probably would have killed Sean had Dan not gotten there in time. Dan shot the leader and Lil Ric took over soon after. Luckily for Sean, Ricardo wasn't there that night and won't know what he looks like.

Jane glances over her shoulders at Sean. She knows he has some history with the ENYM and she's concerned for him. He has a lost look on his face as he drags his feet along behind her. Jane knows this Ricardo fellow is one bad dude. Police have arrested him at least half a dozen times, but he never spent more than a night in jail. He's wanted in fifteen different states for drug and weapon trafficking. And in his spare time, Lil Ric likes to dabble in the black market with other goods and services...

Instead of taking the cruiser, this time they take Sean's Ford F150. Less likely to be called out as police... Then they are on their way...

Chapter 14

The girl found the guy sitting on a couch in the corner of the dance club. He was drinking Champagne and looking bored, despite the hundreds of people dancing around him. There were multi-colored lights twirling about the room and speakers all over the ceiling. Shanna moved toward him with a seductive look on her face.

Realizing that the pretty girl he had been watching was moving toward him, Richard set down his wineglass and winked at her. She was stunning. Her blonde hair shone under the disco balls light, and her green dress made her eyes sparkle brilliantly. She would be his before the night was over; he thought to himself, before she suddenly asked him to dance.

Shanna grabbed Richard's hand and pulled him to the dance floor. She knew he was looking her up and down as she walked in front of him, but she pretended not to notice. He was obviously a jerk, and she hated to have to flirt with him, but if she didn't, the other her would be very upset...

The song was upbeat, and she danced around him sensually. She had to practice an awful lot before she mastered this type of dancing. Her back was to him and she shimmied up and down him as the song progressed. She occasionally filed her fingers through her hair, flinging it from side to side. He was eating it up; it wouldn't be much longer now. He put his hands around her waist and spun her around to face him.

She smiled playfully, and he grinned. "Let's get out of here."

She ran her fingers through his hair and down his spine. "Lead the way."

He gave a short, sinful laugh and threw his arm around her shoulders as he led her to the door. Shanna watched his face as they left, and she giggled. He thinks this is all going the way he planned it, when really, it's the other way around.

Chapter 15

"Remind me again why we dressed like something straight out of a playboy magazine?" Jane asks irritably, trying to pull her very short, black, leather skirt down farther without pulling it too far.

Sean cocks a half smile at her and stalks ahead. "It's not that bad. Besides, if we just came in normal street clothes, Lil Ric could pin us as cops in a heartbeat. They are used to that."

"So, we dressed like hookers instead?" She squeaked.

He turns back, eyeing her up and down. "It had to be as far away from the look of a cop as possible. This is perfect. It looks good on you, though." He adds, while facing forward again.

Jane's cheeks heat up, so she looks down quickly. Other than the skirt, Jane also has on a top that goes only halfway down her stomach and has the word 'SEXY' printed across the front in shiny hot pink letters. She's also sporting some black leather boots that come up to her knees and lacy net tights. She's feeling extremely uncomfortable wearing such revealing clothing, and especially in front of her partner.

Sean trudges ahead of her wearing a white button up dress shirt. He has the top few buttons undone, revealing his broad chest. His watch, a Rolex, shows it's 5:45 p.m. Shiny silver cufflinks hold the cuffs of his shirt down, followed by his designer dark blue jeans that have just enough factory made rips to look both cool and elegant at the same time. He wore black suede shoes with black laces and has his hair slicked back with some expensive gel he'd found in some store he just randomly waltzed into.

They turn into a back alleyway and Sean knocks on a metal door in the brick wall. The door creaks open and a man who looks to be in his late twenties stands in the way with crossed arms. He has blonde hair and gray eyes. His outfit looks a lot like Sean's except for a dark gray sport jacket hanging loosely on his shoulders. "Tony?" His voice growls out.

Sean nods. The man opens the door out wider and moves out of their way. He walks behind them closely and Jane can sense the barrel of a gun pointed at their backs. She tries to keep it together, but she can feel a sense of dread creeping down her spine. Sean glances at her and notices the gun behind them.

"That standard procedure, I suppose?" He calmly questions without so much as flinching.

The gruff man gives him a dirty look but doesn't respond. Jane has the powerful urge to gulp... but she makes eye contact with Sean, who seems to sense her tension and gives her a reassuring look. She fights back the temptation, her shoulders slightly relaxing. The hallway is dark and dusty. Cleaning obviously isn't high on their priority list. They pass several closed doors as they go and Jane wonders what sins are going on behind each. When they finally reach the end of the hall, there are two more men outside of a set of metal double doors. They give Jane and Sean a quick pat down.

Jane squirms uncomfortably as the burly man feels down her sides. She's almost expecting him to try something, but he doesn't. He smirks at her as if to say she wasn't worth his time. She's not sure whether to feel relieved or self-conscious... He finishes and waits for the other guy to finish checking Sean. Once they are both satisfied, they nod to the guy behind Sean and Jane, who lowers his gun and shoves them through the now opening doors.

The two stumble through the doors and the man with the gun follows them in, standing behind them silently. Before them is a set of steps with a chair and desk at the top. There are about three men on either side of the desk. The sides of their sports jackets bulge out slightly, obviously concealing some sizable weapons. They remain emotionless as they stand there with their arms behind their backs. Behind the desk sits an older man, leaned back in the chair, his eyes closed as if asleep.

Without opening his eyes, he snaps his fingers and the two men outside the room shut the doors loudly, causing Jane to jump slightly. Sean gives her another look. He's remaining very calm and apparently thinks she isn't. Can he blame her? She hasn't exactly had the same experience with the mob as he has before this.

Her skirt is riding up in the back and she's tempted to pull it down, but she's too scared to move. She's honestly not sure why they had to frisk her in the first place because her outfit is so tight that if she had a weapon or a wire, they'd know it just by looking.

The old man has salt and pepper hair and a short, well-kept beard. He looks to be of Hispanic descent. Sean recognizes him immediately as Ricardo Bonanno. Technically, he's only half Hispanic. To be a member of the mafia here, you have to be at least half Italian. According to his record, his father was a full blood Italian member of the mob previously. He had a Hispanic mistress whom he had Ricardo with. Ricardo joined after the Irish mafia, a rival mob killed his father in 1990. His uncle was mob boss at the time and made him the underboss. It was his uncle who Dan killed trying to save Sean back in 2011. That was back when Sean was fresh on the force and lead investigator. The Bonanno family is one of the five major mob families in NY. Lil Ric isn't so little anymore... He turns towards them, clasping his hands together.

"So," Ricardo starts, his sharp eyes feel like they are searching their souls, "I hear you're looking for some medication."

He directs the statement to Sean and seems to ignore Jane's presence completely. The room is dark and eerily quiet.

"Yes, sir." Sean nods but says no more.

"Did you have a particular one in mind?" He leans forward, intrigued.

Sean nods, "Well they were talking about one on the news the other day... Said some killer was using it on their victims or something. Seemed to work pretty well for them. Figured it'd work good for, uh, my line of work." He glances over at Jane and winks. Part of the act. "You feel me?"

Ricardo's men squirm a bit and look at him. He keeps his eyes fixed on Sean. Unwavering. "And do you know the name of this medication?"

Sean suddenly looks a little nervous but reluctantly responds, "I think the news said it was called something like quetiapine or something like that."

"Quetiapine?" His eyebrows raise slightly.

"Yeah, that sounds right." He runs his hands through his hair almost subconsciously.

Lil Ric signals to the man behind them, and he opens the door. "Unfortunately, I'm afraid I can't help you. I'm going to have to send you away empty-handed. I wish you the best of luck in finding it, though." He gestures for them to leave, but Jane gets irritated and steps forward.

"Are you saying you aren't the one that sold it to that Judas killer chick? Cause I figured you'd be the best one to go to for stuff like that. Isn't that your business?"

Behind her, Sean moans. She's just made a huge mistake... Ricardo stands up slowly and snaps his fingers. His men rush to detain Sean and Jane. They grasp them and hold their hands behind their backs as Ricardo steps up to them.

"So it is as I suspected? Police I'm assuming?" He pauses for a response. He receives none and continues, "You realize I could have you killed, correct?"

"You don't really want that though, do you?" Sean mutters. "That's not really how you operate, right? You kill us, the police force retaliates, puts a damper on your business that we would have otherwise let be. Correct?" Jane's eyes are wide as she watches Sean practically taunting the mob boss to kill them.

The boss rubs his chin thoughtfully.

"There are exceptions…" He scans their faces for any hint of fear before sighing, "but no. I don't want to do that. I hope you won't force my hand."

"Why not make a deal, then? We need the name of the buyer. What would that be worth to you?" Jane questions and the mafia leader turns to her, slightly amused.

"I'm sure you've heard the phrase, snitches get stitches?" He laughs a little as if he's just made a joke, "I'm not interested in selling out anyone. I'll kindly ask you to leave now. Before I have to break some protocols…" He turns to walk back to his desk, flicking his fingers over his shoulder. The burly men grasping them drag them down the hall and out the front door. Jane struggled against their grip at first, but Sean shook his slowly in warning and she settled down and went with it.

The men shove them away and they both end up face down in the dirt. Sean hops right up and holds a hand out to Jane. She takes it, wiping off the dirt with her free hand on her way up. They make their way back to the truck.

"Well, what now?" Jane mutters and Sean shakes his head in response. Suddenly, out of the shadows, a figure appears, hissing to get their attention.

"Pssstt... Pssstt... over here..."

A shorter, thin, dark-haired boy is hiding between buildings. The two detectives glance at each other nervously before slipping into the dark space with the boy.

He appears to be really young. Not much older than 18. Sean notices the middle finger of his right hand has a small spot of dried blood on it. No doubt this boy was a new member of the mafia. It's their practice to prick the finger of new recruits and wipe the blood on a tarot card of sorts, usually one with the image of a saint on it.

The boy notices Sean's gaze and shoves his hand into his pocket. "Look, I never wanted this..." the boy frowns and peeks around the corner. He's almost shaking with anxiety. "Lil Ric is my grandad. They forced me to join. Look, I need help... I want out. I have the info you need... take me with you? Please? You can announce you arrested me or something... Like say I assaulted you or whatever..."

Jane's face scrunches up. She feels for the kid and wants to help him. Sean gives her a look, but it's too late. She's already nodding. He drags his hand down his face roughly and groans. This is a very dangerous idea. For them and the kid. They come up with a plan and Sean and Jane slide back out of the shadows after peering out to be sure nobody was watching.

They make their way back to the truck and pull out their handcuffs and guns. They put them on as if they were just suiting up in preparation to leave. Suddenly the boy appears. He walks towards them, screaming curse words and shouting "screw you pigs!" Once close enough, he spits at Sean. As Sean wipes spit off his face, fury crossing his features. Jane rushes to apprehend the kid. She gets him in cuffs and shoves him in the back of the vehicle while reading him his rights. A small crowd forms and a bunch of scary looking mafia members crowd around cursing at them. They move as quickly as they can and speed off. Hoping none of them try to follow or shoot at them.

As Sean glances out the back window, he sees the kid in the back seat grinning from ear to ear and tearing up. He glances over at Jane. "You're insane." She simply smiles back at him.

Chapter 16

The lights were beautiful, the way they shimmered against the glassy surface of the table. "Is everything finished?"

There was a moment of confusion across the beautiful blonde's face as she pushed her hair behind her ear and looked up. "I'm sorry?"

Shanna let out a small sigh. "I asked if you finished the cleaning yet." She looked around the room they were in. Her other self was crouched on the floor with tweezers and a boar brush.

"Yeah, I'm just about finished here, then we can leave. There aren't any other rooms or places you went before I got here, are there?" Shanna looked thoughtful for a moment before easing her head from side to side.

"No……no I don't believe so. When we got here, we entered through the front doors and walked down to the hallway straight to this room." She looked up at his body, slowly swaying and moving from some unseen current of air. There was a bright red kiss mark on his cheek. He looked perfect. Not a single hair out of place, but that's just how her other self was. A perfectionist. It wasn't until she looked back down at this perfectionist that she realized her mistake.

"You believe? Either you know or you don't, we're running short on time and I really don't want to scour the entire house for your footprints, fingerprints, or hair. So which is it? Do you believe, or do you know?"

Shanna didn't like the look that was coming across her face. It was scary. "I know." She quickly corrected herself to calm what she knew would be a horrible storm if left unchecked. Her other self was scary, and she didn't like it when she got mad.

The blonde woman before her stared at her until finally Shanna looked away. "I hope you do." Shanna risked peaking back over at her mirror image only to find she was busy putting away her stuff. "I want you to leave now. Take our stuff with you, and please, for pete's sake, watch your step and leave no traces."

Shanna looked down at the bag of tools in her hand. "Of course." She turned and left the room, walking gently in her wrapped shoes, careful of the instructions given to her. She didn't care to be alone. It made her feel exposed, but she knew she would see her other self back at home. That made her feel better on her trip back to the house.

~~~~~

Shanna walked down the stairs of the beautiful estate they called home. She found the other blonde in the kitchen sitting at the table, staring out the window.

Without looking at Shanna, she said, "What are you cooking us for breakfast? We had a long night last night and I'm feeling in the mood for something sweet. Maybe crepes?" She slowly turned and made eye contact.

Shanna shuffled a little uneasily in place. "Crepes sound good. Do you want fruit on yours?"

"Hm, surprise me." She leaned back in her seat and crossed one leg over the other, slowly looking back out the window.

Shanna walked over to the cabinets and began collecting the ingredients for crepes. It was quiet while she worked, no need for conversation. Sometimes she wished for company. Someone other than her other self who would actually have conversations with her, or play a board game. It got lonely when you were by yourself and the only conversations you had were with an emotionless clone of yourself.

Time ticked by slowly as she cooked the crepes, meticulously pouring and spreading the batter. Flipping them as they turned a nice golden hue. When she finished, she spread some whipped cream between each layer with some slices of strawberries and bananas. She stared at the two finished plates and decided she would pour some melted hazelnut spread on top for an added sweetness.

Shanna turned and smiled at her other self, who was still staring out the window. She hadn't moved a muscle. "Here you go, fruit and hazelnut spread. Best combination in the world." Her mirror image looked at the plate set before her. She picked up her fork and gently touched at the fruit and crepes.

With her plate in her hands, Shanna sat down across the table from the other woman. She took her first bite and closed her eyes, enjoying the flavor. She would have loved to have been a baker in another life. Maybe she will be when she gets reincarnated. "Do you believe in reincarnation?" It came out of her mouth before she realized it.

"No."

She peaked up and her other self was still in the same position. Leg crossed over, no emotion on her face and slowly still just picking at the fruit. She hadn't taken a single bite.

Feeling a little braver at the conversation, not being shut down immediately, she decided she would pursue. "Why not? I think that would be nice. After you die, be able to start over with a clean slate." Hearing no response, she perked up a little more. Maybe they could have a genuine conversation that didn't revolve around who their next victim was. "Maybe I could become a baker in my next life. It's fun to make sweets." She looked up with a smile on her face.

Her smile slowly faded as she saw her other's face. It was straight, with no reaction, cold eyes, and a hint of annoyance. "If reincarnation is real, then what's the point in killing these men? They would just be reborn, and who's saying we get a second chance if we are reincarnated? What if we are dealt the same hand? Every.

Single. Time. What a horrible form of entertainment that would be to whichever god is in charge of that. Don't you think?"

Shanna could see the hint of a smile twitching at the blonde woman's lips. She was finding entertainment herself in that thought, Shanna could tell. "Besides, I don't think you would make a talented baker." Shanna felt nauseous. She looked at the plate across from the table from her. Untouched, not a single bite taken. She could see the other woman standing up and walking out of the room as her eyes began to slowly fill with tears.

Her other self interrupted her speaking up again, "Oh, I have our next target." Shanna watched her leave with a smile on her face. She had finished what she intended to do, taken control again. She was always in control.

Chapter 17

Sean walks into the station with the boy in handcuffs. They have to make it look legit. Jane called and tipped off the news media on the way here. Sean glances up at the TV in the station and watches as the reporter on the screen announces the arrest of a 'Bruno Bonanno' with the charges of assault on an officer and resisting arrest. Everyone in the station is staring at him as he walks by, eyes wide.

Captain Marshall appears and blocks his path. "What the heck are you thinking?" He looks seriously ticked off. "Are you trying to start a war? Arresting the grandson of the boss? We do not have the resources to deal with this. And for what? Assault? Please tell me he tried to kill you." He's rubbing his temple, looking quite distressed.

Sean clears his throat to explain, but the boy beats him to it.

"Yo, I got information on this chick you guys are looking for. So I told copper here I'd spill if he'd make it look like he was arresting me and get me out of there. I ain't cut out for that life." The boy looks proud of himself and Sean grimaces, awaiting Marshall's rebuke.

The captain stares at the boy a moment and then meets the detective's eyes again. "Please tell me you did not fake an arrest."

"He spit on me." Sean's shoulders shrug, but he can feel the heat rising to his face.

Dan stares at him as if trying to compute what he's just said before finally muttering, "Get him in an interrogation room. Get as much information out of him as you can. And then call the state marshals. And you better hope for your sake and his that they're willing to take the kid on. If this goes south, I will have your badge for this. I don't know what you were thinking." The captain stomps off, shaking his head. The entire room had gone quiet and Sean could feel eyes staring him down, but he simply nudged the kid forward towards the interrogation room.

~~~~~

When Jane walks into the precinct after parking the car, she notices everyone is looking at her and whispering. She heads up to the front desk and talks to Catherine, the secretary.

"What's going on?" She asks quietly.

"Captain Marshall just laid into Sean in front of everybody. He's pretty mad at you all for bringing in that Bonanno kid. Sean took the heat." Catherine looks uncomfortable and glances over her shoulder. Jane can feel the anger in her cheeks, but she mutters thanks and heads to the interrogation room to look for Sean and the kid.

She finds them in interrogation room b. Sean is scribbling down information as fast as the kid can spit it out. She watches through the glass until Sean finally rises and steps outside, shutting the door quietly behind him.

"Why didn't you tell Marshal it was my idea?" She puts her hands on her hips and demands.

"Because it doesn't matter. We needed the information. Dan will get over it. Besides, I'm the head investigator on this case and therefore, anything that happens is my responsibility. No sense dragging you into it. I let it happen."

He pushes past her, motioning for her to follow. She goes to complain that she doesn't need him to protect her at the precinct or anywhere else actually, but she figures he won't listen. They pass a few people in the hallway, but everyone seems pretty bored with them now. As they round the corner into Sean's office, Jane pops down in an office chair and kicks her feet up on his desk.

"How long do you think it'll be before the Bonannos' show up looking for him? Because you know they will place bail the second his holding time is up. We won't be able to keep him past 24 hours. We'll have to get him in protective services in the next 12 tops. Have you even called them yet?" She barely takes a breath between her bombardment of statements.

A long sigh escapes his lips, and he shakes his head. Walking over to Jane, he places a hand on her shoulder and looks her dead in the eye. "When exactly have I had the chance to do that? I've been questioning the kid since I got done getting chewed out by Dan." He gently pulls at her hand, ushering her out of his seat. "Don't worry, it'll be okay." He flips the page in his notebook and begins jotting down information as quickly as he can before hitting the button on his phone to page someone.

Catherine comes running in and he hands the paper to her. Instructing her to use that information to call the state marshals about putting Bruno in witness protection. He told her not to take no for an answer. She nods nervously and leaves the room.

"So..." Jane clears her throat and starts again, "Did you get anything off the kid that might be helpful?"

Sean glances up at her and passes a page over to her. She reads it carefully as he explains what she's seeing.

"A young blonde chick, maybe late twenties, wearing bright red lipstick came in a few months ago. He said she was wearing a blue sundress and black heels. Couldn't remember any other distinctive markers in her appearance. He also doesn't remember the exact day but thinks it was in March. She was asking for Quetiapine and paid twice the normal going rate for 30g."

"Sounds like our girl." Jane mutters. "And how much have we found in each body?"

Sean pulls out a binder and flips through it meticulously. Finally, he settles on a page and scans it thoroughly. "Looks like about 2g each. 5g would be enough to put someone in a coma and 6g would likely be fatal."

At that, Jane takes a seat across from his desk and holds the paper up, studying it closely, elbows on her knees. "You don't think she bought just enough for the amount of people she plans to kill, do you? Because if we've had 4 bodies so far at 2g per body, that would mean..."

Sean cuts her off. "I don't really want to jump to any conclusions just yet on that. But it's something to keep in mind. But listen, so Bruno said the girl seemed 'off her rocker', his words not mine. Said she kept whispering to herself while she was there."

"Well, we already knew she was probably psychotic since she is using antipsychotics as her drug of choice... along with the fact that she's a serial killer..." Jane rolls her wrist as if this is old news.

Sean nods but still looks deep in thought before moving on to the next topic. "The kid said that his grandfather doesn't really question the buyers unless he suspects them of something. But the way she was talking to herself was freaking him out a little, again his words, so he asked her if they were for herself. He said she laughed and responded 'someone close to me, actually'. He said after she said that her eyes went wide as if she had shared too much information or something."

Jane stands up and paces the floor for a moment. "There were no family connections to the victims, though, right? Like she has no relation to all the victims or even a friend of all the victims... as far as we could find, there was no relation between the victims at all. Aside from living in the same state, that is."

Her partner nods. "That's what I found odd, too. I want to go back and start looking into the family history of each of the victims again."

"Well, most serial killers have a stressor, right? Like they kill people who remind them of someone or something that fascinates them or they want to kill... So what if the person she was referring to hasn't become a victim we've already found but one of the future victims?"

Sean smiles at her, "You learn quick, huh? I hadn't even thought about that. Of course, if that's the case, it still won't help us any sadly. Not yet, anyway..." His smile fades and he runs his hands through his hair. He looks exhausted. Suddenly, the phone rings and he picks it up hesitantly.

"Hello?....... Okay...... Good. Tell them we appreciate it..... alright..... We'll head that way after we deal with the kid. Thanks Catherine."

Jane raises an eyebrow. "I take it state marshals helping with the kid?"

"They said if he's willing to answer a few questions for them too, they are, anyway." He stands and stretches.

"You think he's up for that?" Jane asks curiously.

"I think he doesn't have a choice at this point. Not if he wants to live long. Kid really didn't know what he was getting himself in for... Oh... and they found another body." With that, Sean marches out the door back towards the interrogation room to get Bruno squared away with the marshalls. Jane follows him out swiftly, grabbing her keys off the desk and flipping the light off behind her as she exits.

Chapter 18

Shanna had her white-gloved hands linked through an older gentleman's elbow, pressing her chest against it gently enough that it was noticeable, but not too forward. The lights along the sidewalk flickered slightly as they made their way into the downtown part of the neighborhood. He must be taking her to his friend's house, just as her other self said he would. She knew all along that he would do this. She was smart that way.

They approached a small townhouse that looked as though it was falling apart from the outside, which only meant the inside wasn't any better. She saw him sway a bit as he took a step to unlock the front gate. Good, that meant the first dose of drugs in his drink was already taking effect.

"Watch your step, darlin'." He looked down at her and helped her to walk through the muddy front yard. She was careful not to dirty her shoes. Her other self wouldn't like it if Shanna were to track a lot of dirt into the house. That's more to clean up.

Shanna looked up at him once they made it safely to the front porch. "Thank you." She smiled gently and reached up to run her fingers along his jaw, tracing his growing stubble.

It was hard pretending to be attracted to this man. He was old and had multiple affairs on his wife of 25 years. He's taken many women into his own home, gone to their place, or, as she said, to his friend's house. Shanna was worried that maybe he might not bring her here and that her other self wouldn't be at the right location, but it was useless to worry about that. There were a few times the men brought her to a second location and yet her other self always seemed to be there. Ready and waiting.

He unlocked the door and let her in first. She felt her heart rate racing, a little due to fear, but most from excitement. She was about to take another piece of scum off the Earth. Traitorous men like him shouldn't live. They didn't deserve that right, and just like Judas, she would hang them in shame for the world to know what they did.

The stench of the home cut her thoughts off. Alcohol, sweat, and old food that had been molding in to go containers. She had to hold back a gag that rose in the back of her throat. Her other self was going to have a hard time with this home. Cleaning up the mess would be difficult without over cleaning. Nasty homes were the hardest.

She followed him into a bedroom. The smell wasn't any better in this room, either. It smelled like a frat house after a party filled with too many naked bodies pressed against each other. She could hardly walk across the floor from all the clothes thrown around and the bed was just a mattress laid on the floor with sheets that hadn't been washed since the day they bought them.

She turned around to see him already with his shirt stripped and making his way to unbutton his pants. "You ready to get this started, sweety?" He gave her a smirk, sending shivers down her spine. And not in a good way.

She had to give herself a few more minutes; the drugs had yet to kick in completely. She may need to give him an extra boost. She gave him the best flirtatious smile she could muster; and wrinkled her nose a bit, not able to help it. "Can I go freshen myself up first?" She pointed to where the bathroom door hung open across the hallway.

Apparently, her wrinkled nose didn't phase him any. "Go right ahead. I'll be ready for you." He winked as she turned her back and walked towards the bathroom.

She shut the door and let out a breath, only to be assaulted by the smell of urine. "Ugh, this sucks." Shanna dug around in her purse for the tiny vial and syringe that held the drugs. "Who would bring a lady into this filth? Filthy men, that's who. Don't they realize women enjoy a clean, comfortable space? Even if I was truly here to give him what he wants, he wouldn't be getting it now." She finished filling the syringe with the water and Quetiapine solution that she had readied for tonight.

Shanna honestly didn't know how strong the solution was, but her other self always calculated it properly with how much they would need. Besides, the solution was much stronger than the pills he received in his drink at the bar and with him already showing signs of dizziness, this shot would go straight through and he would be out before he knew it.

"Are you done in there?" She heard the man calling from the other room, irritation ringing through his voice.

"I'm almost done, just a minute more." She looked at herself in the mirror and readied herself for her lips dry and applied her special red lipstick. Her other self made this as well and told her to always use it during their crusades. It would protect her lips from leaving behind too much evidence.

Syringe tucked neatly into her hidden dress pocket, she walked to the door and opened it. She saw him laid in the bed, the door wide open and completely nude. This was one of those moments Shanna was glad her other self taught her how to be an excellent actress. "I'm ready." She smiled at him and walked to the foot of the bed.

His grin looked more like a snarling animal. "Good." With his arms opened up and motioning to her, he said, "Come here."

She walked around to the side of the bed and sat down close to him. He couldn't see the side of her dress that had the needle in it, therefore, he couldn't see her as she pulled it out. She leaned down over him and felt his hands move around her waist. Needing to be quick about this, she placed a gentle kiss on his cheek as she stuck his leg and pushed the syringe.

He jerked away and looked down at his leg, seeing the needle laying in bed. He gazed up at her with a crazed look on his face before he yelled, "What did you do to me?!" He reached out to grab her, but not before she could slip away to the other side of the room.

"It's punishment." If she could keep him talking for just a minute longer, then the booster shot will have its time to work its magic. He was already slurring his words a bit. "How many times have you cheated on her?"

It was a rhetorical question, but he didn't know that. "Cheat on who?" He stood up, staggering to catch his balance on the dresser.

"Your wife." Shanna fought to stay calm and collected. If she let her emotions get the better of her now, then he would too, and she needed as little contact as possible between the two of them right now.

He made his way around the room, stumbling over his own feet. He let out a deep chuckle. "I don't know. Too many to count."

"Why?" She walked around the edge of the room so his back was to the door. When she looked through the open doorway, she saw her other self leaned against the doorframe. Watching quietly at what was happening.

He couldn't pull himself up straight anymore, his eyes drooping, as he became visibly weaker and disoriented. "What did you do to me?" His words came out weak and slurred.

This brought a smile to Shanna's lips, and her other self mirrored her. He was gone. It didn't matter what they did anymore, he wouldn't have the strength to fight them. Without another word, Shanna walked over to him and pulled his face up to look at her. "It doesn't matter anymore."

Standing behind him, her other self handed the end of a noose to Shanna.. She slid it over his head. He reacted a bit, barely able to keep his eyes open. "Waa....s.....at?" His slurred words were hardly audible and his hands twitched at his sides, wanting to reach up and touch whatever was just put around his neck.

Shanna looked at her other self. "We should work fast. He took longer than we planned."

"Of course." She saw her pull on the end of the rope, causing him to topple over without even flinching. The red kiss mark was bright on his cheek from earlier. "I'll get everything ready, make sure to finish with the body."

Shanna felt the weight of a permanent marker in her hand. She knelt beside his still form. He wasn't dead; the quetiapine wasn't strong enough to do that, but he was slipping into a coma-like state. Eventually, after long enough with no medical intervention, he may die from the drugs, his airway closing up and his body absorbing enough of the quetiapine in that time frame to actually kill him, but they didn't have that kind of time.

The alcoholic smell of permanent marker filled her nose when she gently removed the cap. She wrote with a careful hand so as not to mess up. She would be in trouble if she did that. JUDAS. It was perfect. She smiled to herself.

When she looked up, she saw the other her standing there, watching. There was an eye hook in the ceiling that wasn't there a moment ago. Most likely where there was a ceiling joist to hold his weight. She made eye contact with the other woman and knew it was time to begin. Standing up, she handed the end of the rope to her other self, and she made her way back to the body to lift him into a sitting position.

She never saw her twin help with the physical work. In fact, most of the time Shanna never saw her doing any of the work at all, unless it was cleaning. Things just happened and Shanna knew it was her other self doing it. Like the marker in her hand, or the eye hook in the ceiling. Just like now, lifting the body, her other self was behind her somewhere. Surely she was pulling the end of the rope along with her to lift the body. There was no way Shanna could do it by herself, right? When she turned around, she was alone. She knew her other self had to have helped, though.

After she had the end tied off and secure, she stepped back to look at their work. The ceilings in this house were low, but still tall enough for his feet to barely dangle above the floor. His hands and feet twitched as the rope constricted his throat and he fully lost consciousness due to lack of air.

Her other self stepped forward and picked up some of their supplies. "Let's hurry and get this place cleaned. I can't stand this smell for one more minute."

Shanna giggled, thinking back to when she first stepped into the house. The stench was awful.

Chapter 19

Sean fills out paperwork as quickly as he can. Two state marshals wait patiently for him to finish and then take the clipboard from him. Sean glances over at the kid sitting on a couch across the room talking with another marshal. He makes eye contact with Sean but there is no smile. He looks scared. The detective sighs.

"Take care of the kid, alright?" He says, rubbing the back of his head nervously.

"We have it under control, detective. Let us do our job. We've done this more times than you can count." The marshal pats Sean on the shoulder, but it's less reassuring and more demeaning. Sean twists so the marshals' hand falls off his shoulder.

"Alright then, hop to it. His family will come around soon enough and you all need to be gone by then. And I've got a murder to get to, if you'll excuse me."

Sean brushes past them and heads for the door. He's about the push on the metal bar to open the heavy glass door when the sound of his name being shouted reaches his ears.

"Sean!"

He recognizes the voice instantly and groans before turning to face Dan.

"Sir?"

Dan narrows his eyes. "Sean, did you just moan when I called you?"

"Yes, sir." There's really no point lying to him when he heard it.

"And you don't feel that's a disrespectful way to respond to your superior?" Dan looks somewhat bewildered and Sean lets out a low, deep breath.

"Sir, I have a crime scene to get to." He responds. His answer came out slowly, taking care to not upset Dan anymore.

This time Dan sighs. "Fine. But I expect you in my office when you get back."

Sean steps aside as the marshals and Bruno exit. Dan watches them leave and then faces Sean again. "You better be pretty thankful they were willing to take that kid on... Now get to the crime scene and I'll see you back here after. Immediately after. You hear?"

Sean nods and bolts out the front door. Jane is already waiting in the car out front as he slides in. He glances up at the sky out the windshield as he plops down.

"Looks like it may rain." He mutters, placing his elbow on the window frame and his head against his hand.

"Oh, no way. The weather? Really Sean? What happened there? I saw Dan stop you at the door." Jane twists around in her seat to confront him.

He groans again and says nothing.

She raises an eyebrow. "Well, I certainly hope you didn't react that way to him…"

Sean looks away, rubbing his forehead. Jane's eyes widened.

"Oh, my gosh, you did! Didn't you?! What were you thinking?" She stares at him as small drops of rain sprinkle against the windshield.

"I wasn't. I'm just tired." He leans back and turns to look out his window, watching the rain slowly picking up. "I'm worried about the kid, We didn't really get any more information than we already had and now there's another murder, I just don't feel like I'm doing any good… And then Dan expects me to be doing good… I guess I just feel like I'm not living up to everybody's expectations. And in our line of work we can't really afford to not meet expectations…" He goes silent for a few moments and looks suddenly embarrassed, his face turning a slight shade of pink. "I'm sorry. I don't know why I'm spilling all this on you…"

His partner watches him with what appears to be pity and… something else. He stares into her amber eyes for a moment, trying to read her mind somehow. Does she think he's less of a man for sharing his feelings like that? Is she considering finding a more competent partner? Or does she understand? But then, how could she? She's still basically a rookie. Nobody is placing all that responsibility on her. But then what is that look she's giving him?

Jane reaches over and rubs his arm gently. Sean jumps slightly at her touch but tries to hide it as she speaks. "We'll solve this and catch whoever it is. The marshals will get Bruno to safety. And Dan... Dan will calm down. It'll all work out, eventually. And I... I believe in you. You're a great cop, and I know you will figure it all out." She suddenly blushes and pulls her hand away from him, placing it back on the wheel. "We should probably get to the crime scene before they think we've gone AWOL or something."

He nods, but can't seem to form any response. His arm still feels somewhat tingly from where she rubbed it, and he's trying to assess the situation. Jane changed the subject back to the weather, mumbling about turning on the lights and complaining about the wipers being worn out. She has her midnight black hair pulled up in a long ponytail behind her, but a bit of bangs keep sliding into her eyes. She tries to blow the hair from her face and growls as she fails miserably. He reaches over and tucks it behind her ear for her. And at that, her face goes from pink to scarlet. He pulls his hand back quickly and turns forward again. The rain is getting harder and Sean is more confused than he's been in a long time.

What exactly just happened?

They sit quietly the rest of the way to the crime scene. Jane's face slowly returns to its normal shade as they pull up the driveway. Sean barely let the car stop before flinging the door open and hopping out. Another officer greets him and points the way into the house, following behind him and spilling information.

"The house belongs to a 'John Carson' who discovered the body."

Sean glances at the officer behind him in surprise. "You mean he wasn't the victim?"

The officer shakes his head and continues, "Carson says the victim is his friend. Apparently The victim had permission from Carson to bring women here. The guy says he's hardly ever home, as he apparently lives with a girlfriend most of the time. They had a fight last night, and he came home. Found the body this morning."

"He came home last night but didn't find the body till this morning?" They round the corner into a large room and find the body hanging from the ceiling. The room smells of sweat, bleach, and fireball. Not a delightful combination. Sean's nose crinkles at the stench.

"Apparently after the fight, before coming home, he went to a bar… And was not fully present when he returned home. The guy says he passed out in the living room on the floor as soon as he walked through the door. Didn't make it back here to the bedroom until this afternoon when he had finally slept it all off." The other officer makes some faces too, as the smell hits him while he talks.

Jane enters the room silently, holding her nose. Sean glances at her and then quickly turns away again. He doesn't want things to be awkward between them, but he's not really sure how to avoid that after whatever that was in the car on the way here.

As he walks into the room, Sean notices an interesting difference in this crime scene compared to the others. This man is naked. He glances back at Jane and notices her trying to avoid looking at the victims closely. He contemplated making a joke about her reaction to a man's naked body, but then he suddenly remembered the interaction in the vehicle and his face blushed again.

Choosing to remain silent instead, he circles the body, seeing the usual, aside from the lack of clothing which appeared to be discarded nearby. Nothing out of the ordinary from what he can tell.

"Did anyone swab for vaginal fluid? If he's naked this time, do we think it went that far?" Sean asks forensics.

"Nothing. It was the first thing we did." One of them responds.

"What's that on his shoe?" Jane suddenly speaks up from across the room. She rushes over and kneels down next to a pair of black leather dress shoes on the floor near the bed. Sean steps over beside her and leans down, looking over her shoulder. The man's shoes don't appear out of the ordinary to Sean at first glance. One is laying on the floor upright while the other is laying on its side. It's obvious he kicked them off in a hurry. But as his partner points to the tread on the bottom of the one on its side, he notices right away what she's referring to. The bottom of his shoe has specs of something pink and sparkly in the creases.

"Is that glitter?" He quickly motions for the other officer to bring him a bag for the man's shoes.

Jane nods and steps away to allow them to work. She whispers to Sean, "This is the first time we've found some evidence on the body, isn't it? If the killer was wearing some kind of glitter, they've never left it behind before... Do you think they're getting careless? Or do you think the glitter was from something else?"

Sean shakes his head, deep in thought. "I'm not sure. But it's definitely a fresh development... Where's the man's vehicle?"

The other officer that had brought Sean to the room turns to face him. "I believe it's still out in the driveway. The friend said he was too drunk to notice it when he got home but that he recognized it as his friends when he ran outside screaming after finding the body."

"I want forensics searching it for other signs of this glitter and anything else that might give us some clue whether it came from the killer or somewhere else." Sean says and the officer nods and rushes from the room. He then looks at his partner and runs his hand through his hair nervously. "I don't think there's anything else we can do here. They have it under control... And Dan wants me back ASAP. Apparently, we have a meeting scheduled..."

Jane scrunches her eyebrows in concern but nods, digging her keys out of her pocket and following him out the door.

Chapter 20

Shanna stretched out across her bed, staring at the curtains above her. Her room was immaculate, the way her other self likes it, but still showed hints of her own personality throughout it. She loved green. It matched her eyes, and her room was full of deep emerald green. She had shimmery green curtains that encased her bed.

It made her feel like a princess.

She had her bed covered in decorative pillows, some the same green as the curtains that hung from her windows and bed, others a metallic gold with hints of emerald colored designs running through them. She loved her room. It was the only space in the house that she felt like herself.

It had been three days since she saw the other woman last. She honestly didn't know where she went most days, only to appear when the target was ready.

As she stared at the shimmery green cloth, her mind wandered, going blank. The shimmers danced in the soft yellow light and almost looked like stars from another world that was shrouded in green. She was losing herself again.

With a shake, Shanna sat up and looked around the room, coming back from the scary parts of her mind that she tried to stay away from. It wasn't easy. She could feel those dark thoughts getting closer every day, the ones the other woman gave into and lived in. She didn't want to become her.

She stood, her nightgown swishing around her, brushing the carpeted floor of her room. She made her way through the house, looking for something, anything. There was no tv or phones. No internet or game consoles. The other woman didn't like those things. She was paranoid.

The house itself was startling white as she walked through it. The only contrast was the dark hardwood floors. Her other self was obsessed with white. It was perfect, and untouched. She had plans to remove the old flooring and replace it with white tiling. It had to be spotless, though, no other color streaking through it.

She went to the kitchen, the faint smell of butter and eggs from breakfast that morning still lingered. The kitchen was also that stark white. White cabinets, white backsplash and countertops, even the appliances were pure white. Again, the only contrast being the dark hardwood flooring.

Maybe she could have a snack? As she searched the cupboards, her boredom reached a new high. There was nothing good to snack on and there was nothing fun to do in the house.

She briefly entertained the idea of going outside only to dismiss those thoughts. Going outside alone was out of the question. If her other self found out, then she.... She didn't want to think about what would happen.

She found herself standing in the massive room at the front door. There was a beautiful set of stairs right in the middle, and bits of a faint memory tickled at the back of her mind. A movie she watched as a child was barely there. She couldn't remember much from then, but images of girls sliding down massive stairs on a mattress. They were laughing, and it looked fun.

Before she could change her mind, she rushed up the stairs, two at a time. She made her way to one of the spare bedrooms. She was expecting it to smell musty and unused, but of course she should know better than that. Her other self always kept everything perfect, and she was thankful for that as she ripped the sheets off the mattress and dust didn't fly in her face.

The pile of sheets on the floor made her pause for a moment. She would be in trouble if she couldn't make it look exactly as it had before. Her anxiety rose as she stared at the mess she made. Her feet froze in place as those dark thoughts climbed into the back of her mind again. However, before they could take over, the image of the girls, faces twisted in laughter and joy, flashed across her memory again.

The mattress wasn't large, just a twin size, so it wasn't heavy as she dragged it across the hardwood floors in the hallways. Little creaks sounding between the soft scraping of the mattress. She pulled the mattress to the very edge of the stairs and sat on it.

A strange feeling of excitement ran through her as she stared over the edge, teetering back and forth. This felt different from what she felt during her crusades. It bubbled down deep inside of her, overflowing into a grin that spread wider as the mattress finally tipped in favor of the stairs.

A squeal escapes her lips as the air whipped past her, causing her hair to fly around her, stinging her in the face. She felt every bounce of the steps jar through her, causing her laughter to bounce up and down. As quickly as it began, it ended. She slowly came to a stop in front of the front doors.

She turned her head to the side and saw her reflection in the giant mirror that hung on the wall. She liked what she saw. Her blonde mane whipped around her face from the wind and her eyes were bright with something she didn't remember ever being there before. Joy.

"Did you enjoy yourself?"

Her twin materialized out of nowhere, standing behind her in their reflection.

She couldn't answer, her voice stuck in the back of her throat. She felt the darkness in her mind take hold. Strangling all her thoughts, restricting them to nothing but fear.

"I hope it was worth it." Her voice darkened as she took a slow step towards Shanna.

Shanna couldn't bring herself to turn around and face the other woman. Her heart raced and her eyes no longer reflected the joy she felt earlier, they only showed fear now. Fear that ran deep and caused her body to shiver uncontrollably. "I'm sorry." It came out as a tiny squeak, barely audible.

"I didn't hear you." Another step. "You know I don't like it when you don't speak clearly." Her voice was calm, but the venom in each word sent another wave of fear through Shanna.

"I'm sorry. I'll put it all back the way it was." She spoke louder now. Her words spilled over each other, hoping that she could calm her twin before she reached her.

Another step.

"I was just bored, and it looked fun. I didn't mean any harm!" Her breath came quicker.

Another step.

"I'm really sorry!" Her words were now coming out between wracking sobs. "I swear I'll never do it again!" Her cries came out harder.

Another step. She was now directly behind Shanna, towering over where she still sat on the mattress.

"Please." Another whispered cry.

"I said to speak clearly." She stared, no emotion showing on her face, just burning rage deep in her eyes. The darkness finally took hold of everything Shanna knew was her. It was these moments that scared her. She couldn't ever remember what exactly happened during those times, but she always woke up terrified, feeling deep in her bones something bad had happened.

~~~~~

When Shanna woke again, she had no way of knowing how much time had passed. She wasn't in her room, just on a cot in a solid white box of space, shivering from the cold. It was freezing, wherever she was, and her stomach gnawed in hunger, making her weak. She was slowly gaining consciousness and remembered why she was there. It was her punishment for having fun. She laid there, starved and freezing, her fingers tinged purple and her head pounding from starvation.

She tried to sit up, but was too weak to get very far. She stayed propped on her side by her elbow as her eyes drifted to a corner of the room where she sat.

"Are you better now?" Her voice hinted that she needed to answer correctly or her punishment wouldn't end there.

"Yes." Shanna's voice was loud, startling her for a moment.

"Good." I would hate to have to punish you more. It interferes with our plans, you know. Again, her voice darkened into something that made Shanna shiver even more.

"What happened this time?" She hurt all over and she could see hints of bruises peeking out from under her nightgown. As always, they were in places that weren't visible when she dressed to greet the men.

"If you don't remember, then you don't need to know."

Shanna stared at the floor, waiting for her other self to leave. When Shanna felt her presence gone, she finally looked back up, the spotless room disorienting her for a minute.

She laid there for a while longer, trying to get the strength to stand up and leave. She needed to eat something so that she could feel better. Did she deserve to feel better, though? She was punished for having fun. She deserved this pain and hunger. It was proof she had done wrong and was bad. It was a lesson she was supposed to learn.

It took her a minute to decide that she gave permission to leave. If the key was there, then she was right. She stood in front of the door and reached to the top of the framing. There it was, cold and hard under her fingers. She unlocked the door and stared at the steps in front of her that led up to their house.

She made her way back to the world of the living, one step at a time, she climbed the stairs.

Chapter 21

They ride back to the precinct in silence as the rain pounds on the windshield outside. It's coming down so hard you can barely see the road at this point. Jane is driving slower than she wanted to, but maybe that's a good thing for Sean. After all, the quicker they get back to the precinct, the quicker he gets yelled at. After their emotional connection on the way to the crime scene, she wants to help him relax a little. Give him a chance to collect his thoughts... And for her to collect hers.

She's always thought he was good looking, but something about hearing him pouring his heart out to her caused some kind of deeper emotion to stir. She's not sure what to make of it and she knows that acting upon it would be in violation of police department rules. So now she has this feeling that she doesn't know what to do with. Has it always been there? Somewhere just deep down buried underneath her own insecurity? Perhaps hearing him so vulnerable and insecure himself caused her to open up that walled up area of her heart... What a time to do it though when it's against regulation. This can only end in more pain for the both of them.

~~~~~

They finally pull into the parking lot and she tries to get as close to the door as possible. Sean nods his head at her in thanks as she drops him off by the front awning. He holds an arm above his head as he rushes from the vehicle to the door and disappears through the opening, the glass door swinging shut behind him.

Sean knocks on Dan's door softly.

"Come in."

He pulls the door open just enough to slide his body through and shuts it behind him. Dan is behind his desk, typing hurriedly on the computer. Sean marches up and plops himself into a chair. Dan glances up at him curiously and then shifts his gaze back to the computer screen.

"Well," Sean starts, "Am I fired? Demoted? Written up? Or am I just here for another lecture?" He asks.

Dan stops typing and gives him a look that seems to say 'have you lost your mind?' And at this point Sean is wondering the same thing. It seems he's had no control over his mouth today. As if whatever he thinks just bursts out with no filter. Perhaps it's the lack of sleep? Who knows, but it's most likely about to get him in a lot of trouble.

"Are you okay Sean?" There is genuine concern in his boss's eyes. Sean's taken aback, not sure how to respond to this as he was expecting a reprimand.

"I don't know. I would like to say as well as expected. But then, I'm not sure what is expected." Sean sighs and leans back in his chair, rubbing his temples.

Dan looks at him with one eyebrow raised. "I know you, Sean. Something's wrong. And it's affecting your work."

'Here comes that lecture...' Sean thanks to himself.

Dan continues, "Look, I know I'm your boss... But I'm also your friend. We've known each other a long time and I can tell that this case is really getting to you. And yes, I need you to push through it. Because these victims, this town, need you to figure it out. But I care. So what do you need from me? I'll do what I can to help. But you've got to run things by me before you do them."

Not saying anything, Sean just nods. Studying Dan's eyes for any hint of what he'll say next.

"The kid's family stopped by. We told them we had released him and we didn't know where he went after. Thought you would want to know." Dan grabs a stack of papers, staples them together, and hands them across to Sean. "And here's the transcripts from your interview with him... from the looks of it, I take it you didn't get any information you didn't already know?"

"No..." Sean mutters dejectedly, hanging his head.

"Well... It is what it is. Any luck at the crime scene? Anything new there?" He asks, changing the subject.

Sean looks up and nods, regaining a little composure. "He was naked... And there was glitter on his shoe. I'm having forensics look into it."

Dan's eyes widen a bit, and a small grin appears on his face briefly. Sean can't help but grin a little too at Dan's reaction to the word naked. His boss goes to say something, but suddenly the phone rings. He grabs it and pulls it to his ear.

"This is Captain Marshall." His face suddenly goes ashen white. "This soon?"

Sean stands up, stepping closer and mouthing, 'What is it?' at him. His boss ignores him, focusing on the phone call.

"I see." He glances up at Sean as he finishes the call. "I'll let him know. Expect them in an hour, tops."

Sean raises his eyebrow as Captain Dan hangs up the phone and slowly returns it to its stand.

"What's going on?"

"We have another body." Dan says. He sits back in his chair, a sign escaping his lips.

"But it hasn't even been a day since the last!" Alarm ringing in Sean's voice.

"It's old. They said decay puts it around about a week. Apparently, this one happened between the last one and the one before. But it still means they're getting closer together... go get your partner and let her know you're heading back out. I'll text the coordinates to your phone." Dan stands and walks with Sean to the door.

"We'll head straight there." Sean nods at Dan as he pulls the door open and rushes through.

Dan grabs it and leans out, yelling to stop him, "Sean!"

Sean stops and glances back at him.

"You be careful in that rain. And... I'm serious about letting me know if you need something. I need you at your best. So if there's something I can do to help you get there, let me know."

Sean nods without a word and rushes off to find his partner.

~~~~~

Jane was just coming in when Sean found her and explained the situation and they both ran back out the door. They are both back in the car and on their way there. It's still pouring rain and Jane can feel her stomach growling. As soon as they leave this scene, they will have to stop and get something to eat. She can't remember the last time she had eaten.

They pull up at a small trailer and before she even has the car in park, some screaming woman is racing at their vehicle. She knocks on the passenger window and Sean jumps slightly. He pushes the door open slowly, giving the woman time to move out of his way as he slips out. Jane shuts off the ignition and pockets the keys, climbing out herself.

"When are these people going to be done with my house? Are you the one in charge here?" The woman gestures wildly at the crime scene. Sean looks flabbergasted and somewhat intimidated by the female. Jane slides up beside him and addresses the woman.

"We are. Was the victim related to you?"

The woman places her hands on her hips and huffs. She smells of smoke and has bags under both eyes. If

Jane were to judge by appearance, she might consider drugs playing a part in this woman's irrational outburst.

"Yes. It's my no good cheating husband. And I'm guessing you're gonna wanna question me since he's dead and I obviously have some kind of motive, right?. Ask whatever you want but I didn't kill him. And I want these people out of my house." She hisses.

'This woman is something else...' Jane thinks to herself. But Sean responds first.

"We actually have a few questions. But it's not because you're a suspect. We're afraid your husband was the next victim in a slew of murders. We need to know if you had any idea where he was about this time last week. Or if you recognize any of these names." He pulls out a list of the other victims' names and passes it over to her. She glances at it briefly and hands it back, shaking her head.

"No idea. But then I wouldn't know if he knew them or not. The slimeball cheated regularly and was rarely home. I was on a business trip all last week and I came home today to find this. The kinds of people he hangs out with it was only a matter of time before he wound up dead." There isn't a tear or even a hint of sadness in her voice.

Jane clears her throat and asks, "So you wouldn't know where he might have been a week ago, then? They put the time of death about five days ago. Would have been during your, uh, business trip."

The woman brushes some loose hairs out of her face and narrows her eyes at Jane. "Between the bars and strip joints, your guess is as good as mine. And that last sentence of yours sounded awfully accusing. What exactly are you trying to insinuate?"

Jane's mouth opens slightly, as if she's considering how to respond, but before she can Sean looks as if a light bulb just went off in his head and speaks up.

"Strip joints you say? He frequent those?"

The lady turns back to meet Sean's eyes and nods. "When he's not screwing around with some whore down the street, then yeah, he likes to get his rocks off at the strip joints. Two in particular are his favorites, the one on 45th Street and the one on Broadway."

Jane suddenly understands where Sean is going with this and whispers in his ear, "You thinking that's where the glitter came from on our last victim?" He nods at her and then thanks the widow.

"We appreciate the help, ma'am. We'll have this wrapped up as quickly as possible. If you can think of anything else or if you need anything, be sure to call the precinct and ask for detective Fenton."

She confirms she will and Sean and Jane head into the house. As they're walking in, Sean pulls out his cell phone and calls the station. "Hello, Catherine? Will you please call the strip club on Broadway and the strip club on 45th and ask them if we can swing by after this and pick up their security tapes for the past couple of months? ……. Thanks, just text me with what they say…….. I appreciate it. Bye."

"This could be our big break in the case…" Jane says and grabs Sean's arm in excitement. He startles a little, glancing down at her arm linked with his. He slowly and gently pulls away from her and gives her a smile, running his fingers through his hair.

"Could be… Here's hoping."

Chapter 22

The smell of alcohol filled the air as she made her way into the changing rooms. Her heels clicked across the old linoleum floors, where girls were caking on layers of makeup and glitter. Perfume spritzing and misting the air with tiny droplets, only making it that much harder to breathe in the already stuffy space.

"Hey Delilah, you're up in a minute on stage. Get ready." Sheila, the house mom, stood in the doorway watching her girls get ready. Her best girl had just walked through the door and was due on stage.

The blonde beauty gave the large woman a curt nod and walked to a vanity. She spoke as little as possible. She was here for a job and a job only.

Sheila shook her head, dark curls bouncing around her face. She knew better than to expect a response. Her girl would be on stage with no issues. She was good like that.

The blonde stared at herself in the mirror for a moment before reaching for her makeup. Her name wasn't Delilah, of course. That was just her club name. Her persona she put on as a means to an end. Glitter shimmered across her body as she stroked her shoulders with a makeup brush.

Today she went with white, it was perfect, untouched. She unbuttoned her top to reveal her bikini she would dance in and made her way backstage. She faintly heard the DJ call her name and music began vibrating the ground under her feet. The UV lights showed off her bikini as she grabbed the pole and slowly made her way around it.

Her focus was somewhere else, though. Her eyes landed on a man seated only a few feet away. He eyed her up and down as she stared at him. Watching her as she slid down the pole in time to the music.

She knew who he was. Charles Jeffers. 32 years old, married, one child. Multiple affairs in the past year alone. He came every Saturday, right on time.

A smirk spread across her face as she maintained eye contact with him. His mouth curled up with desire while he stretched back in his seat, legs spreading wide. He picked up a glass of cheap alcohol and took a slow drink, trying too hard at some form of seduction.

The woman took slow, deliberate steps across the stage. Her hips swaying in time to the music as she teased at the edge of her bikini bottom. She could tell from the glint in his eye she had him hooked. This would be a piece of cake.

~~~~~

Sheila watched as Delilah made her way back into the changing room. "Good work out there. You made a pretty penny today."

The only response she received was a smirk.

Sometimes Sheila wondered why they ever hired the girl. She was gorgeous, Sheila couldn't argue with that, but they didn't even know her real name. She claims Delilah, her stage name, is her real name, but Sheila knew better. Girls didn't come into this field using their real name.

She brought in money, though. The customers always flocked on her nights, the numbers spoke that loud and clear. Sheila watched as the dancers moved around, some taking off their makeup from the night, others just putting it on. The body glitter and highlight making them all shimmer and glow. Delilah stood out from them all. She had an authority about her that commanded attention and Sheila herself had a hard time ignoring it.

A tall red head made her way through the vanities to where Delilah stood. "Hey girl, how's your week been?" She plopped into the chair next to where Delilah sat, draping her legs over the arm.

Delilah barely glanced over where the lanky girl sat. "Better than yours, I'm sure." She leaned forward in her seat, closer to the mirror to reapply her lipstick. She didn't know why Cherry liked to talk to her every time they worked together. Most people didn't like to talk to her, and that's the way she preferred it.

"Ugh." Cherry threw her head back and let out a breath. "Probably. My week sucked. My boyfriend went off on me again about my job before I came in on Wednesday and it ended up being this whole thing."

Delilah made no remark. Her earlier comment wasn't an invitation to a conversation, and responding now would only get Cherry talking more.

"Not to mention my rent went up and my car has taken this wonderful moment to act up. I'm gonna have to pull a couple more days this week just till I figure something out." She sat up and put her feet back on the ground. "Good news, though. My friend is getting married and I'm gonna be her maid of honor. I'm 'supes excited."

Again, the blonde chose not to respond. She picked through her curls, perfecting each one.

Cherry watched Delilah meticulously move things around on her station and touch up her hair and makeup. She must be slightly OCD or something. She had everything lined up by color, size, and function. Not to mention she never had a single hair out of place. "What's your deal?"

Delilah stopped picking at her hair and just stared at herself in the mirror. What's her deal? Did she really just ask her that? If it weren't for the house mom choosing that moment to call Cherry on stage, Delilah may have made a comment that wouldn't have been wise.

Delilah watched as Cherry walked away in her tall platforms, "I'm so ready to be done here." She still had most of the night to go before she could head home. Hopefully, she could make it.

Chapter 23

Jane could hear the base the second she opened the car door. The music in the strip club is blaring as they make their way up to the front of the line.

"ID?" A burly man with crossed arms huffs at her and before she can respond, Sean reaches over her shoulder and holds up his badge. She quickly pulls hers out and flashes it as well. The doorman scowls but pushes the big metal door open and ushers them in.

Jane's nose wrinkles up as the smell of sweat and smoke hits it. Red and yellow lights flash around the room and the music is so loud she can barely hear herself think. She glances back at her partner to find him staring off to their left. Following his gaze, her eyes land on a tall, slender woman with dark hair and hardly any clothes sauntering in their direction. Her eyes narrow.

"Hello handsome." The woman purrs as she steps up to Sean, inches from his face. "Can I help you with something?"

Jane can feel the heat rising in her cheeks and she clears her throat to get the woman's attention. "Yes actually. We're here from the police department, on official business. We called." The woman flips her hair back with her hand out of her face and slowly turns her attention to Jane. Her eyes run up and down Jane's body, causing her to become even more uncomfortable than she was moments earlier. The woman's gaze lingers over each part of her as if sizing her up and Jane feels the sudden urge to put on even more clothing...

Sean's face is red as he runs his fingers through his hair and takes a slow step back, trying to make it unnoticeable. "Can you please take us to whoever would be in charge of getting us the security tapes?"

The woman sighs and nods her head towards a door off to the side. "I have to get back to work. But you'll find Sheila through there." Then she turns and sashays away. Sean's eyes instinctively follow and he suddenly feels his partner grab his arm and pull him towards the door. He almost trips from the force of her pull. A twinge of guilt rises in him as he turns back to Jane and notices her face. She looks frustrated... but something in her eyes looks... almost sad. He's not sure why, but he almost feels like he's done something wrong to her somehow. He hangs his head and clears his throat.

"Sheila must be the one I spoke to on the phone. Let's get these tapes and get back before it gets too late. We have a lot of film to go through..."

Jane lets go of his arm and nods, leading him through the door. He avoids the temptation to glance back behind him again and keeps his eyes steady ahead. He's beyond ready for this day to be over.

On the other side of the door, they find a small office. The walls are a bright yellow and covered in black and white photos of girls in various positions on stage. It's hard to tell from the photos what color their hair is, so Jane doesn't waste her time with them. There's a dark-haired woman sitting behind the desk counting money, a cigarette sticking out of the corner of her mouth.

"Smoking is a pretty unattractive habit, you know?" Jane plops down in an empty mushroom chair in front of the woman's desk.

The woman raises her eyes to glance at Jane without moving from her position. "So I've been told. And you are?" She smirks, wrapping a rubber band around a wad of cash and placing it inside the top drawer of her desk.

"Are you Sheila? The manager?" Jane leans forward, glancing at some of the loose paperwork on the woman's desk.

The woman sighs and looks up at her fully. Her eyes give Jane a once over before turning and doing the same with Sean, who has been silent since they entered.

"I am. But if you're here for a job, I've got enough girls right now. You and your pimp should try the club across town. I hear they just lost someone." She grins maliciously, "Of course, I wouldn't know anything about that..."

Jane scowls and starts protesting, but before she can, Sean steps up and flashes his badge.

Sheila's smirk drops and she nods. "My bad. I suppose you're the ones who called for the videos then..."

She stands up and walks over to a filing cabinet, opens it, and pulls out a box of DVDs. Walking back over, she holds the box out to Sean, who takes it and mutters thanks. Then she turns her attention back to Jane.

"You should take it as a compliment, honey. You've got the body for this line of work if you ever wanted to pursue it."

Heat rushes to Jane's face as she stands to leave. But she still can't help but glance at Sean to see his reaction. Her partner has his head turned ever so slightly and is looking at her in a way he's never looked at her before.

"Let's go!" She says forcefully, breaking the awkward silence.

He seems to snap out of it and nods. Following her out the door, letting it swing shut behind them.

~~~~~

Sean places the box in the backseat and heads around to the passenger side.

"Hey..." Jane calls over the hood to get his attention and he turns to look at her. "I know I usually drive... But would you mind this time?"

"Uh, sure..." He holds his hands up to catch the keys as she tosses them through the air. As they meet switching sides, she mutters a quick thank you and he nods.

Driving back, the car is eerily silent for a while. Suddenly Jane lets out an exasperated moan, taking Sean by such surprise that he almost jerks the wheel a little but catches himself.

"Can you believe she said that to me? To us?" She has one hand rubbing her temple as if she has a headache.

"Well, we did just pretend to be a hooker and a pimp recently. Maybe we just have a hard time getting out of character after going undercover?" It was a sorry attempt at humor and doesn't surprise Sean when he gets a glare in response.

"It was a joke..." he mutters, "but I don't know... maybe you should take it as a compliment. I mean, you are just as beautiful as any of those girls in there. Probably more since you actually have some self respect."

He glances over at her and the look on her face lets him know he might have just opened a door he didn't intend to. He tries to shrug it off, like it's no big deal, but it doesn't work.

"You think I'm beautiful?" Her voice cracks slightly, and Sean realizes this conversation is not one he can handle while driving. He pulls over into a nearby parking lot.

It's late, and the business is closed for the day. The lone street light gives off a faded glow. Sean puts the car in park, leans his head back against the seat, and sighs. After a moment of silence, he turns to find her still staring at him. Waiting for his response.

"Jane I... if we... you know..." He's not sure how to have this conversation. Staring into her eyes, he can see a few tears threatening to well up. The last thing he wants is for her to think that he doesn't feel the way he feels... But at the same time, he knows the rules would never allow them to be together. What would this even accomplish?

"Yes. You're beautiful." His head drops, and he looks away from her, towards the bottom of the steering wheel.

"I... I find you attractive as well..." she whispers.

Sean groans softly, turning towards her. "Jane, I just don't think..."

He starts, but before he can finish, she leaps towards him and plants her lips against his. He grabs both her arms, every intention of pushing her back, but then he stops. Suddenly, all those brief looks made sense. Maybe he was just scared to admit it to himself... but he has feelings for Jane. His heart is racing in his chest as he decides to just accept the chemistry between them. His hands slide up her arms, over her shoulders, and eventually embrace the back of her head, pulling her in closer.

After a few moments, they pull away, their breaths heavy.

Sean stares into his partner's eyes, taking in the brilliance of their gold flecks.

"This is not a good idea... The department..."

She shakes her head. "It shouldn't be up to them."

"But it is... the rules... we..." He can sense her tense up as she slowly leans back to her side. He doesn't want to hurt her. Maybe they never should have opened this door. Maybe it was all a huge mistake. But... "We're gonna have to keep it hidden..."

Her face lights up and he can't help but smile. He can't believe this is happening. What are they thinking?

Chapter 24

The sound of Shanna's knife, thumping against the wooden cutting board, filled the empty spaces of the kitchen. The tomato juiced across the board as she carefully made a few more slices for the sandwiches.

Just in case.

Today was going to be a good day, she could tell. Everything was in place for the new victim. Her outfit was perfect and so was her mood. She began humming a tune she couldn't place words to. It was something she remembers her mom used to sing to her as she fell asleep at night.

She laid her sandwich, perfectly prepared, on her plate, and a second one unassembled on another. She had to make sure nothing on the plate was touching, in case she didn't want something on the sandwich that day.

"What are you thinking about?"

Shanna jumped a bit at the noise. It sounded loud in the quiet space, even though it was barely more than a whisper. "I was thinking about that nursery song mom used to sing us. What was it again?"

There was no response.

Shanna turned around and the other her in the doorway to the kitchen. She was staring at Shanna's plate. "I can hum it for you if that would help you remember. I can't remember the words, though."

Her eyes drifted away from the plate to stare back into Shanna's. "Why does it matter?"

"Well, I miss mom, and I keep forgetting things. Things I would like to remember. Maybe you can help me. You were there too, remember?"

A smile played at the edges of her lips as she continued to stare, looking straight through Shanna. "I remember as much as you do, Shanna." The smile hinted at something a little more than comfort.

"I guess that would be true, wouldn't it? You were there with me. If I can't remember, then I guess it would make sense that maybe you couldn't either." She responded.

"Remember that next time you think to ask questions about mom. Or dad." She was no longer smiling, just staring at Shanna's plate again. "Remember, tonight we're going to Terry's Bar. He should be there. It's the weekend, and he had a hard time at work this past week."

She took one last look at Shanna's plate before turning and disappearing into the house.

Shanna set her plate down on the counter and let out a shaky breath. Maybe today wasn't meant to be such a good day after all.

~~~~~

Shanna walked down the sidewalk, about a block away from Terry's. It was dark out, well into the night, and few people were out. A shiver ran through her. Even though it was still summer, technically, the nights were turning chilly. Tonight more so than others and this only made Shanna even more nervous. Something about tonight was off.

She continued to put one foot in front of the other, her heels clacking quietly. It didn't matter if she wanted to go home tonight and wait until another day. Her other self wouldn't let her. It had to be now. Everything was perfect and set up. There was no turning back.

She shuddered again, the uneasiness of the night trying to find its way out.

Terry's neon sign blinked in the distance, inviting stragglers in for the night, promises of something other than what they can find back at their homes. Perfect for the type of men that Shanna took care of.

The door stood there, uninviting to her at that moment and she had to take a deep breath before heading in. Warm, humid air flowed past her as the hinges creaked under the weight of their movement.

She really didn't want to be there tonight.

Shanna made her way to the bar, her dress shimmering in the low lights. The smell of alcohol made her want to gag, but she knew better. She had to keep up the appearance.

The alcohol had her on edge.

Her brows furrowed a bit. What was wrong with her tonight? There was something playing at the edges of her memory. She didn't like it either. She saw her man sitting at a table, suit undone with a can in his hand as though he's given up on the world. He was watching the news on the Tv in the corner.

The bartender made her way to where Shanna was sitting. "What can I get you?"

"Just a glass of water, please." She said.

The lady eyed Shanna up and down, "Alright." A few seconds later, she came back with a glass and placed it on the bar. "Just let me know if I can get you anything else."

"I will, thank you." She spun the glass around for a second before taking a sip. She waited a moment for the bartender to walk away and assist another drinker before turning her attention back to her man, Charles.

She stood and went to take a step in his direction, drink in hand. It wasn't a long distance, but her feet were dragging, still being weighed down by her sense of dread.

She paused for a second.

Charles was still watching the news, his red hair showing signs of aging. Must be from stress. He's still so young.

She took another step.

Each step became harder as she drew closer and the sound of the TV filled her ears, becoming unbearable.

She shouldn't be here tonight.

This was the first night that she ever felt a sense of doubt, as though the plan was going to go awry and not work. Something was going to go wrong.

"Hello." She smiled down at the man where he sat. "May I sit here?" She asked.

He turned his attention from the TV and let a dark grin spread across his features. "I don't mind one bit."

She took a seat next to him, placing her glass down.

"Well, that's no fun. Can I get you something a little stronger than that?" He said. His breath stretched across the small span of space, irritating Shanna's uneasiness even more.

Another memory.

"I can have plenty of fun with just water." She was doing her best not to show her nervousness.

"Good, good." He said. He leaned back and took another drink, talking to himself as his imagination worked double time, taking in the young lady in front of him. "Good."

Shanna smiled and glanced up at the TV. "Anything good in the news?"

He let out a bark of laughter. "Yeah, some sicko is finally getting out of prison."

"Really?" she asked.

"Yeah, something about raping a woman or some other crap." He took another drink as Shanna turned her attention to the newswoman on TV. "Pervs like that deserve to rot in hell."

"They do, don't they?" She mused.

The woman on TV droned on, "Judge has passed his ruling, setting free Steve Michaels after 10 years."

Shanna's hands went cold, the blood draining from her face as she stared at the screen, unable to breathe properly. She heard Charles vaguely talking in the background.

"That prick didn't deserve to get out. Like I said, deserves to rot in hell. People like that should have it done right back to 'em and then thrown in the electric chair." He growled.

Shanna slowly stood, bracing herself on the table, not trusting her legs. Charles kept talking, eyes on the TV, not seeing the reaction Shanna was having. She backed up, bumping into her chair.

Charles must have finally noticed her cause she heard him speak, the sounds muffled in her ears. He touched her arm, drawing her attention back towards him. "You alright?"

She jerked away. "Don't touch me!" Her voice shrilled out, grating against her own ears. Her breaths became shorter and shorter. "NO!" She turned and made her way through the few people there watching as she rushed by.

"No, no no no no no no." The words were barely coming out as she whispered with each step, fighting something clawing inside of her. She made her way down block after block, taking turns, her mind reeling.

"No, it can't be dad." She said.

She bumped into a stranger making their way down the street. They threw profanities her way, but she didn't hear them. "He's not out. He's not out."

She kept going.

"It's impossible, it's not time."

She stopped, not sure where she was. As she glanced up, she saw her other self standing there. Furious.

What if she finds out? What is she going to make Shanna do? She didn't know if she could kill her own father. She wanted to stay home and ride a mattress down the stairs again.

"What are you doing? Why did you not bring him?" She stood there, an imposing wall, impossible to bring down.

Shanna's breath caught in her throat again, words barely croaking out. "He's out....... I'm sorry...." The other her hovered closer, becoming more towering as the seconds passed. "I...I'll.... I'll go back." Shanna took a step back.

"What did you say?" She asked. Her voice was too calm.

"I'll go back." Her breaths kept catching in the back of her throat, causing her words to come out small and weak.

"No, before that."

"He's out."

"Who."

"Dad."

"He's not our dad anymore!" She snapped, her face contorting and going feral for a second.

Shanna shuffled back a few more steps, almost tripping over her heels. "mean...St...Steve."

"Where's Charles?" Her words growled out.

"In the bar." She said.

"Why?"

The figure consumed Shanna in front of her, overwhelming her, making it harder to breathe and sending chills through her. "I'm sorry." Her small words filled the space and lingered.

The other her moved back and, as though nothing had happened, fixed her face to show nothing again. She turned and walked off, heading away, going home. Shanna followed and reached up to brush her face, noticing the tears that streaked her cheeks.

Chapter 25

The sky is darkening out as Sean walks down the street, hands in his pockets. A cool breeze blows through and he shudders slightly. He stops in front of a small church just a couple of miles from his apartment.

This is the reason he went for a walk tonight. He's passed by this church every day for the past 20-odd years, but he's never been in it. Tonight, he had finally worked up the nerve to try it.

But maybe not while other people were in there...

He waited and watched as people filed out of the building. Leaving after the evening service. It's about 7pm, Sunday evening and the church sign says the service started at 5:30. Sean lets most of the people move from the front doors before bounding up the steps and slipping through the door. Pulling his hat from his head, he makes his way down the now empty aisle towards the altar. Behind the wooden bench, there's a large cross hanging on the back wall. Soft pink lights illuminate the iconic symbol.

Sean stares at it a moment and then awkwardly attempts to kneel.

"Um..." he mutters and moves his hands in the shape of a cross in front of him. Unsure of what he was doing. Nearby, someone clears their throat, and he nearly falls over, startled. Glancing to his left, he notices a man in black dress pants and a white button-down shirt. He had a striped red tie around his neck and a pair of reading glances on. The man was grinning at him and Sean stood to his feet, running his hand through his hair.

"Sorry... I just... did I do the cross thing wrong?" He asks.

The man shook his head, "Looked good to me. But then again, I don't suppose I'd know any better than you..."

Sean frowns and hesitates for a moment, "Oh... I just assumed you were... So you aren't the priest, then?"

Now the man let out a slight chuckle and held out his hand for Sean to shake. He took it.

"Pastor Benjamin Odell. But you can call me Brother Ben. And I'm afraid you've stumbled into a Baptist church, my friend. Were you raised Catholic?"

Sean glanced back up at the cross a moment as he let go of the pastor's hand. "I'm not really sure. I guess, I remember people doing that hand thing but it's been a long time... Y'all don't do that here?"

"No. But if it makes you more comfortable, I won't stop you. What brings you here tonight?" The pastor gestures to a pew behind them and they both sit.

"I don't really know. Or well... I guess it's more that I can't talk about it... I'm a police officer and a case we are working on has me reconsidering some things I used to... um... consider?" He speaks.

Brother Ben stares, a smile playing on his lips before he responds, "I see... The Lord has a strange way of getting our attention sometimes, doesn't He?"

"You have no idea. Anyway," Sean stands up and his eyes shift back towards the door. "I can't really stay long. I just wanted to..." He trails off.

"Hmm... Well, the good thing is... if you came looking for God, you don't have to stay long to find Him. He was with you when you came in and He'll be with you when you leave. But if you ever have the time to stick around a bit, I'd be happy to help you look." The pastor smiles and stands to his feet, patting Sean on the back reassuringly.

Sean feels tears burning at the back of his eyes. He nods and thanks the pastor, heading back towards the door. Before pushing it open, though, he turns back a moment. "Maybe when this case is closed... Maybe I'll have more time to come back..."

Brother Ben smiles warmly. "I'll be here. The good Lord is willing anyway."

'The good Lord willing', Sean thinks as he trudges back out into the night.

Chapter 26

"It's okay. It's okay, all okay." She mumbles to herself. The little girl rocks back and forth in the dark corner of her closet. Hands covering her ears from the screams coming through the cracked door.

"I know you've been running around with other men! I work all day long only to be treated like *this*!" Her father is bellowing, words almost indecipherable.

She muffles a cry, trembling at the thought that he might hear her. Her mother didn't reply. She didn't have to, though. He wouldn't believe her, anyway. He never did.

The screaming continues. He must have been drinking. She cautiously peeks through the cracks of the closet doors. Light barely filters through, showing all the dust specks floating around in the tight space. All she can see is his back, blocking her view of her mom just on the other side.

"Please, Steve" Her mom's voice was weak. She would have missed it had she not been listening. "I swear, I've been home all day."

"Like I could believe a whore like you." He spat.

The young girl saw her father pick up a bottle from the nightstand and hurl it towards the wall behind her mom. "Like I could ever believe you!" He roared. The alcohol in his system only fueled his rage and made him even more delirious.

The little girl saw his body tremble, fists clenched as he continued to yell and accuse her mom of things she never did.

"She didn't do it." The little girl mumbled to herself, wanting to tell her father her mom was telling the truth. She had been home all day with her. They baked cookies, planted a few flowers in the garden, and even played in the backyard for a few hours. All the proof was there. "She was with me." She whimpered.

"Shh."

Her head jerked, curls flying, as she looked into the darkness on the other side of the closet.

"He'll hear." It was a soft whisper.

She was here too. How could she forget? Squeezing her eyes shut and putting her hands over her ears, she blocked the world out again. She couldn't get her in trouble, either.

Her rocking continued.

The world blocked out as she continued to silently cry, not moving to wipe her tears, afraid she'll make more noise. More glass shattered, this time closer to her refuge.

This time, she wasn't able to cover her squeak fast enough.

Without warning, the closet doors flung open. Her father stared down at her. Eyes blazing and face red. "There you are." he said.

"No!" She saw her mom's hands grab at his shirt, pulling. "You're mad at me, remember?"

"Shut up, Leah!" He shoved her away, reaching down, picking the little girl up by the collar of her dress.

She shrieked. "Mom!" Her little fingers wrapped around his wrist, pulling. Fighting to free herself as her feet kicked against the carpeted floor.

"I cheated on you! Remember? Isn't that why you're mad?" Her mom's sobs shook her whole body as she tried, desperately, to put herself between her daughter and husband.

He flung the girl down, spinning around to grab her mom by the neck. "I *knew* it." He hissed. His entire body was tense. Shaking as the veins in his arms and neck bulged. "*I knew it*!" He screamed. Spit flying in her mom's face as he shook her in his grip.

The little girl scrambled back, tripping over her own feet as she made her way back into the closet. The doors closed behind her as she sobbed and covered her ears, once again, rocking with her head between her knees.

"I told you to stay quiet." The quiet voice whispered once again.

Chapter 27

"We have been here for hours…" Jane is laying on her back on top of Sean's desk with her head hanging over the side. Her long black hair doesn't quite touch the floor. She stares at the TV upside down. Sean is sitting on the floor off to her left. He's surrounded by case files and photographs.

"At least we narrowed it down to the one club." He rests his head back against the desk and turns to look at Jane. When he does, their faces are so close and she can feel his hot breath on her nose.

"Ahem."

The sound of someone clearing their throat in the doorway startles them both. Sean leaps to his feet and Jane, in an attempt to get up quickly, falls off the side of the desk. She stumbles up right and faces the door to find Captain Marshall there. He narrowed his eyes at them in what looks like a cross between concern and suspicion. Jane inwardly groans, realizing that explaining the previous scene will probably be difficult.

"Am I interrupting something?" Dan glances between Sean and Jane curiously.

"No sir. We've been combing through the surveillance tapes all night. We've narrowed it down to one club that all the victims appear to have frequented at some point..." Sean hands the Captain a pamphlet for the strip club on 45th Street, The Emerald Eye.

Marshall glances at the paper briefly, but then turns his attention back to Jane. "May I ask why you were lying on the desk, detective?"

Jane tries to shrug nonchalantly, but she can feel a little heat rising into her cheekbones. "It's the closest thing to a bed in the office... we've been here all night... I was tired and wanted to lie down. It won't happen again."

He nods slowly, unsure about leaving the conversation that way but deciding it wasn't worth it at the moment. "See to it that it doesn't." He glances at Sean. "Do you understand?"

Now Sean's face is bright red and Jane gets the feeling that his threat may not only be referring to her sleeping on the desk... She ducks her head as Sean attempts to change the subject.

"Yes. As far as the case goes, we're now thinking that maybe the killer works at the strip club. Possibly one of the... uh... dancers." His eyes drift over to Jane briefly and she notices a small grin forming on the edges of her lips.

It's cute that he's nervous about upsetting her, she thinks.

"So can we figure out which dancer or staff member had contact with every single one of our victims at some point?" Dan nods towards the tv.

"Working on that." Jane chimes in, "there's just so much footage and really several girls could be suspects... These men were there on multiple nights with multiple girls. It's just a lot to comb through."

"Right, well, I'll let you get back to it. Let me know if you find anything. It's been 3 days since the last kill and we're all getting a little antsy... She's due." The captain turns to leave as Sean and Jane nod in agreement.

~~~~~

It's a little while later, and Sean leans back in his chair, sighing. "I think we need to talk to the manager there again. We can get a list of all the girls that work for her that have blonde hair, maybe?" Sean rubs his chin thoughtfully.

His partner is sitting across the room in a metal chair, a large piece of pizza in her hand. They were starving but had to order delivery so they could keep working. He looks down at the paper in his hand. A list of descriptions of all the girls who had been with all the victims at least once on camera. It was a long list.

"Wouldn't hurt to get the names of the girls on the list either... considering all we have right now is a description of their underwear and wigs." Jane responds, peeling a pepperoni off of her pizza and tossing it in her mouth. He doesn't understand why she separates it like that.

He nods and stands up. Jane gives him a funny look, and she pulls the pizza back from her mouth and questions, "Wait? Are we going right now?"

She goes to get up, but Sean shakes his head.

"No. We don't need to go back there until we're ready to arrest somebody. If we keep going in, we're going to scare her off... I was thinking we could use my computer and video chat with her instead." He saunters around the side of his desk and moves the mouse to wake up his computer screen. A moment later, it's ringing.

His partner hops up and heads over just as Sheila's face appears. She looks annoyed.

"I take it you found something?" She's writing in a notebook and barely glances up at us.

"Yes ma'am. All of our victims frequented your establishment before their deaths. How many girls that work for you have blonde hair, you know, under their wigs?" Sean watches as Sheila huffs and puts down her pencil.

"Um..." Her eyes dart around as if she's counting before she continues, "4 currently."

"And their names?" Jane jumps in, picking up a pen and paper so that she can take down the information.

"Honey, Sassy, Lexi, and Delilah." The woman on the other side of the screen picks up a Betty Boop coffee mug and takes a sip of whatever's inside.

Jane furrows her brow in frustration. But Sean beats her to the reply.

"Ma'am, we're going to need their legal names. Not just their stage names." His eyes narrow as Sheila drags the coffee mug away from her face, looking guilty.

She clears her throat, places the mug down, and runs her hand down her face as if preparing for a tough conversation. "I'm afraid I don't have that information..." she said.

"What? What do you mean you don't have that information?" Jane leans forward on her hands in front of the monitor.

The woman groans and places a hand against her forehead. "Look, the truth is... sometimes girls come in off the street out of horrible situations and need a place to go. A place that doesn't ask questions... I don't ask questions, I just help them. I give them a job and a paycheck and a new name. And that's the extent of it..."

"And that would be illegal!" Jane yells, and Shawn gently grabs her arm and pulls her away from the monitor. He rubs her lower arm a little until she calms down and lets out a deep breath. She walks around the desk towards the pizza box across the room.

"Am I going to need a lawyer?" When Sean looks back at the screen, Sheila is nonchalantly applying lipstick as some kind of coping mechanism.

"I will tell you what, you help us catch our serial killer and start doing the proper paperwork and background checks from this point on, and we will overlook it up till now. Does that sound fair?" He replied.

Sheila hesitates with a nervous frown, but then nods in agreement.

"Good. Since you don't have any information on the girls outside of work, can you at least give us a description of what each girl wears during her shift?" Sean reaches over and pulls the papers with the description of the girls from the videotapes closer.

"Not much..." Jane says it almost in a whisper across the room, but Sean hears it. He grins and shakes his head softly, glancing up over his computer at her.

"Yes, of course." The voice from the computer replies, "Well, Honey is blonde on stage as well. She uses her natural hair. Her ensemble is gold with fringe."

Sean checks the list and doesn't see that description on there, so he nods for Sheila to go on.

"Sassy wears red on stage. Sometimes it's a one piece, sometimes two... She uses temporary hair dye to make her hair Scarlet red."

There's a girl fitting that description on the list and Sean circles it, writing "Sassy" in the margins. He nods for her to continue.

"Lexi wears a black wig and a sparkly purple two-piece. And Delilah wears a white two piece and her natural hair."

Both of the girls are on the list and Sean marks them.

"Well, we've narrowed it down to three then..." He reads back over the list and suddenly thinks of something. "Ma'am? Do the girls pick their own stage names?"

Sheila looks surprised by the question, but nods. "Yes, they have to pick their own name. Usually it's something food related or another name they've always liked or something..."

"What are you thinking?" Jane puts down the piece of pizza in her hand and walks over to look at the paper with him.

He points to Delilah's name as she reads over his shoulder. "If I'm remembering correctly, Delilah is another name from the Bible. I'm pretty sure she was the one who tricked Samson into giving up his strength..."

"So you're thinking that our killer may have stuck with the biblical deceiver thing at her day job, too?" Jane's voice raises an octave and Sean can tell that she thinks he's onto something. He sets up a little straighter, feeling good about this lead.

"Exactly." He turns back to the screen. "Does Delilah happen to wear any kind of body glitter at work?"

"Um," the woman places a finger to her chin thoughtfully. "Yeah, several of the girls do. Though they all usually choose different colors if they can to make their act more distinct... But yes. Delilah uses pink glitter."

Sean glances at Jane, and she's already giving him a knowing look.

"When is Delilah's next shift?" he asks.

Sheila quickly stands up and opens the door behind her, rummaging through several files. She finally pulls one out and tosses it on her desk. Flipping through the pages, she quickly finds the one she's looking for and runs her finger down it. "She's supposed to be working tonight. She should have been here a few hours ago. I haven't been out on the floor since I got here today, but someone would have come and told me if she didn't show..."

"When does she get off?" Sean stands up to grab his keys.

"She's off in an hour."

"Thanks." He clicks the 'end call' button and turns to Jane, who's already waiting by the door.

Chapter 28

Delilah steps down the stairs, heals clacking against the worn wood. Her shift finally ended, and she's ready to head home and get clean. As she sits in front of the mirror, slowly cleaning makeup and glitter off, she can't help but think about the next potential victim.

After the screw up with Charles, this one had to be perfect. She can see Cherry making her way through the other girls in the room towards her and slowly lets out a breath.

"Hey girl." Cherry comes into view, turns and leans against Delilah's desk.

Delilah ignores her, clenching her teeth as she continues to wipe her foundation off her neck.

"So you seriously have to teach me some of your moves." Cherry looks down at the top of the desk and scans the items placed neatly in rows. "Like, I watched you finish up just a second ago, and I swear it was almost too perfect."

Delilah continued to wipe shoulders down, removing some of the glitter.

"How do you do it?" Cherry looks back up at her. "I'm in some serious need of cash right now and if you just, like, showed me a couple of your moves, it would be fire."

Delilah glanced up at Cherry, still making no remark.

Cherry looked back down at the desk, her eyes landing on a tube of mascara. She reached down nervously and picked it up. "I mean, I'm sure you're super busy and what not, but maybe you could just tell me how you learned them or....." her voice trailed off.

She sat there, watching Cherry pick up the tube and clenched the arms of her chair. "Go."

Cherry froze and looked back at her. "Huh?"

"Who said you could touch my things? Get off of my desk, put my makeup back down, and go." She locked eyes with Cherry and through clenched teeth added, "Please."

"Chill." She placed the mascara back where it belonged and stood up. "I forgot you're like, OCD or something, my bad." She walked off, giving up on trying to get lessons at that moment.

Delilah let out a long breath and slowly tried to regain her composure. She hated people. They liked to touch things that didn't belong to them, messing up the order and placement. Everything has its place.

She moved the tube just a fraction back to its original spot.

That's right, everything can be perfect so long as they all remain in their place.

She stood and put her regular clothes on over her work clothes. She would finish cleaning up at home, as much as she hated leaving with glitter still on her. It would get everywhere in the vehicle and in her room, but she couldn't stand to be there a moment longer.

It was at that moment that Sheila found time to poke her head out of her office and call for her, "Hey, Delilah, can I speak with you for a second?" she asked.

She looked over at Sheila and began making her way to her. "I guess."

Once she got into the office, Sheila shut the door behind her and made her way around the room, back behind her desk. She sat down and looked up at Delilah, still standing by the door. "Please, sit down."

"I don't plan on staying long. What did you need me for?"

Sheila glanced over at the clock hanging on the wall and then back towards Delilah, her foot gently bouncing up and down under the desk. "Well, I was wondering if you'd be able to pull more hours this upcoming week for me."

Delilah didn't care to hide the look of disgust that crossed her face. "No, thanks."

"Are you sure? We could really use the extra income and I would even up your percentage for those days to make it worth your time." She glanced back at the clock, foot still tapping.

Delilah stood there, quiet for some time. Shelia couldn't help but be a little tense when in a room alone with Delilah. She was intimidating and in a way that most people wouldn't be able to put a finger on why. Although, after hearing the detective's suspicion of Delilah, she was beginning to understand.

"Again, I'd rather not." Sheila was antsy, she could tell. About what she wasn't sure, but she didn't like that it was involving her. "If you're short on cash, I'm sure Cherry wouldn't mind taking on extra hours. She was just telling me how she needed more income."

Sheila sighed and rubbed her eyes, "I guess I could ask Cherry... It's just your one of our best, no, you are our best and so I know there would be more money coming in if it were you." The tension in the room was pressing down on Sheila in a way that was making it harder to breathe.

"I'm leaving. I'm already tired of being here and this did not help my mood any." Delilah turned to leave.

Sheila glanced back up at the clock. That should be enough, surely. She hated doing this, but it couldn't be helped. If Delilah really had any part to play in the recent murders, then she didn't want that in her club. She watched Delilah walk out; the door clicking softly shut behind her and finally relaxed some.

After shutting the door behind her, Delilah grabbed her bag and quickly headed for the back door. She felt the hairs on the back of her neck stand up as she reached for the doorknob and paused for a moment. Everything about what had just happened with Sheila wasn't sitting right with her.

~~~~~

Shanna sat inside the black Trans Am, checking her face in the mirror, when she heard someone yelling from outside the vehicle. It took a moment to realize the yelling was being directed at her.

"Step out of the vehicle with your hands up!"

She opened the door and stepped out. The red glow of the club's neon signs lit up, revealing a pair of officers, both guns pointed in her direction.

"Put your hands up!"

She stood like a deer in headlights and locked eyes with the female officer that kept yelling at her. Her arms slowly reached above her head, trembling as the warmth of tears ran down her cheeks.

"Put your hands behind your head!"

It didn't take long for her to realize what was happening. A choking sob passed her lips, and she jumped as the female officer's voice hit her ears again.

"I said put your hands behind your head!"

She could hardly control her arms as her body began to violently shake from fear. Her hands reached to the back of her head and her sobs came louder.

She didn't even notice the male officer as he came up and twisted her arms behind her, forcing a yelp out as she felt her face hit the cold hood of the Trans Am.

She could tell he was speaking to her as metal scraped her wrists, cinching tight and pinching. She couldn't hear him, though. All she could hear was the convulsing gasps as she cried and shook against her vehicle.

The door creaked as it opened and she stepped out into the fresh night air, almost peaceful, except for the scene that she saw playing out before her at the opening of the alley.

"I said put your hands behind your head!" A dark-haired female officer had her arms outstretched, a gun in hand, pointing at someone. Her partner standing next to her, mirroring her stance.

Delilah wouldn't have thought anything strange of it, it wouldn't have been the first time police arrested someone in front of the club... Except today she saw Shanna standing next to the Trans Am, hands going behind her head and her face twisted in fear with tears streaming.

She could hear her sobs all the way down the alley, only for them to be cut off as the male officer grabbed her arms and slammed her against the vehicle.

Delilah stepped back, trying to hide in the shadows, but she couldn't bring herself to look away, or even turn and run back inside.

The male officer put Shanna in handcuffs and Delilah couldn't register what was being said anymore.

"You have the right to remain silent, anything you say can and will be held against you in the court of law." He said.

She continued to back up, tuning out what was happening in front of her. This was okay. She didn't need Shanna to finish the job. After she messed up with Charles, Shanna wasn't reliable anymore, anyway. But then… Shanna is the only one left who she somewhat cares about. And it is pretty frustrating that this happened just before they were about to finish it all…

She felt something stiff brush the back of her legs and turned to look. Just the dumpster… She quickly hid behind the other side and slid to the ground, still listening to the cries of her sister as she was being drug to the police vehicle.

Also, she couldn't have Shanna taken away. What if she ratted her out? Surely not. She knew how important it was for them to finish what they started.

A car door slammed shut.

But Shanna was weak. She wouldn't be able to lie to them for long.

Two more car doors.

She needed to hurry before they caught on. They obviously were able to track down her place of work, and that meant it was only a matter of time before they were to find her, too.

She heard the car pull out, and the night went eerily silent in its place. All she could hear was her breathing rhythmically puffing in the frosty night air.

She sat for a moment more, stunned and still processing, unsure of whether she should move or not.

The sound of the back door opening was her answer. She held her breath and listened for the sound of someone leaving, but that never came. Instead, she heard a sigh and Sheila's voice, "Thank God." The door clicked shut and again, quiet fell upon her.

Chapter 29

The girl sitting across the table from Jane in the interrogation room hasn't stopped crying since they picked her up. It's hard to imagine this emotional young lady could have hurt anyone. She honestly seems like the person who cries when they run over a frog on the road... And currently she's in hysterics, sobbing and mumbling and shouting.

"You don't understand! GAH!" She slams her hands down on the table and then goes back to crying again. Jane holds back a groan. She's so ready for Sean to get back. He took the girl's fingerprint down to have it compared to the one they found on the victim's shoes.

"She is going to be so mad... You don't understand what you've done!" She screams and then mumbles to herself softly, barely loud enough to hear, "They don't know what they've done... She won't like this... the other me... I mean... yeah she..."

'This girl is crazy...' thinks Jane. Luckily, the door swings open at that moment and Sean marches in. He pulls the other chair out from under the table and plops down by Jane, giving her a small nod.

"Okay, I'm detective Fenton and this is my partner, detective Masters. Can you calm down long enough to tell us your real name?"

Jane can hear a small bite in his tone and it doesn't much match his usual demeanor. The print must be a match... That has to be the reason for his anger.

The girl stops crying almost immediately and looks at him. She studies him quietly for a moment and then asks, "Are you married?"

Sean's eyebrow raises, and he glances at Jane as if looking for assistance. "No." He states.

The girl narrows her eyes. "Have you ever been?"

Sean shifts uncomfortably. "No. Shouldn't we be doing the questioning?" He glances at Jane again and this time the young woman across the table follows his gaze.

Jane tries hard not to show any emotion, but the heat is already rising to her face. She reaches down and grabs her bottle of water off the floor and takes a quick sip. The blonde tilts her head in consideration and her eyes dart back and forth between them briefly.

She knows. Jane can tell. And Sean must be worried about it too, because he turns and glances at the mirror behind him. The captain must be in the observation room, Jane thought. Great... their careers might just be in the hands of a serial killer right now. Sean attempts to change the subject before that can happen...

"You see miss, your fingerprint matches a ---"

She cuts him off. "I don't want to talk to you."

Sean looks a little surprised and annoyed. "Well, you don't exactly have much of a say in that unless you would like to wait for a lawyer."

"I don't want a lawyer. And I don't want to talk to you." Her eyes drift back to Jane. "I'll talk to her. Not you."

"But I..." Sean attempts to protest, but a knock on the wall signals for him to stand down. He bites the inside of his mouth. "Fine." He gives Jane an encouraging look and hands her the file before he leaves, making his way to the observation room next door.

Jane squirms in her seat anxiously and opens the file before her. "So... your name?"

"Shanna." she replies.

"Is there a last name to go with that?"

"Um, I don't think she would want me to tell you that yet..."

Jane raises an eyebrow at her. "And she is?"

"The other me."

"Right..." Jane is sure this girl is suffering from some kind of multiple personality thing or something, so she plays along for the moment, "Of course... Shanna, your fingerprint matches the print we got off a victim. Do you recognize this man?" Jane pushes a picture towards her and the girl glances at it, almost uninterested.

"Of course. The gambler. He wasn't nice. She told me."

"The other you, I'm guessing?" Jane asks.

Shanna nods.

"And did you kill him?" Jane leans forward.

"She and I."

Jane glances back at the mirror before turning back around. "Right... So you confess then?"

Shanna shrugs, "I don't see why not. But you really should let me go now if that's all you needed... She won't be happy. You probably won't like how she reacts..."

Pulling out the rest of the victims' photos, Jane spreads them out in front of Shanna. "Yeah, I understand. But what about these?"

"I don't really think you *do* understand though..." Shanna huffs in frustration. "They were all horrible and didn't deserve to live. But now I don't really know what she will do. I mean, until time for the last thing. She might go crazy... We're supposed to do the last thing together, you know?"

"I think we are long past crazy here, sweetheart. But how were you able to lift these men by yourself?"

"By myself?" Shanna looks really confused and gets quiet, as if processing this statement. As if thinking, 'Had she been by herself?'

Jane's limited knowledge of dissociative personality disorder would warn her not to break the girl's delusions abruptly. She needs to see a shrink or something to do this gradually... but Jane needs a full confession and explanation to close the case. She just doesn't have time to feed into this girl's fantasy.

Suddenly, as if on cue, the door bursts open. Sean enters in a panic and ushers Jane out.

"Um, stay here Shanna." Jane grabs the file and rushes out, letting the door shut behind her.

The phones ringing off the hooks all the way down the hall is all Jane can hear. Sean and Captain Marshall both have pale faces as they turn to her.

"There's been another murder... actually, from what we can tell, there's been two. Just since the time we left the club with her." Sean informs Jane, his stomach turning circles.

"What? But... how? Her fingerprints match!?" Jane's eyes widened.

"It gets weirder." Captain Marshall states, "The MO is basically the same as our killer, but the lipstick is on the opposite side and now it's in blue. Also, they aren't strung up anymore, but they were just found laying on the ground with a rope around their neck. We thought maybe a copycat, but for one, they still have the same meds in their system and for two... they dusted for prints at both scenes and ran them right away and... They match Shanna."

"But how's that..." Jane gasps, "Oh my gosh... she's not crazy..." She then runs back into the interrogation room. "Shanna!" She shouts as she enters, Sean and Dan right on her heels, "When you said the other you did you mean your sister?"

"Yeah. Although she doesn't like me to call her that... I was supposed to pick her up from work so we could go get the next bad guy. She's not going to be happy. We are the same age and look the same and stuff, but she gets a lot angrier than I do. You really ought to let me go now."

"Shanna, honey, I need to know your sister's name. Please. It's important."

"She told me not to tell anyone her real name. She prefers her stage name Delilah..."

"We need your last name. Um... your sister might be in danger; do you understand? If we want to help her before she gets herself hurt, we need to know a few things. Can you help us?"

The girl looks like she's thinking it over and then slowly nods. "If it'll help her. You can't tell her I told you, though! Promise?"

"Promise".

"I need an APB put out on a blonde-haired female last seen covered in pink glitter leaving the strip club. She's probably wearing a dress of some sort, likely revealing. Goes by the name Delilah. Here's a list of all the potential victims still on her list, but we believe her primary target is Steve Michaels, her father, who's just been released from prison." The Captain is yelling to the entire station as he passes a picture of Shanna over the counter. "Get this picture out to all the local news stations and tell them the suspect is this one's twin. I want the city warned to stay inside. Sean!"

Sean rushes over with Jane right behind. "Yes, sir?"

"I called the prison, and they had an address for Michaels. I need you and Masters there now!"

"We're on it!"

Chapter 30

Her hair whipped in the wind as she walked out onto the front porch of the second victim's house. He was easy to take care of. Already asleep, all she had to do was give a nice dose of the drug to keep him that way. The one before him was easy too, too messy, but still easy.

He was still awake, in a back alley, drunk. All she had to do was get close enough to give him the right dose to kill him. Of course, she remembered to put a noose around his neck and a kiss on his cheek. Couldn't have people thinking he got away with his crimes.

Her heels from work clacked along the sidewalk as she walked with purpose. Closing her eyes for a moment and taking a deep breath, all she could think was '*one more*'.

After watching Shanna get arrested, Delilah felt something snap inside of her. Almost like that last piece of string holding the rope together, keeping her from falling over the edge of the cliff.

Here she was, falling, and it felt amazing. No need to worry about things being perfect. They weren't anymore.

Those officers ruined that. A grimace crossed her face as she thought about that. It angered her to know that they were so close, things were so close to being perfect.

Gritting her teeth, she climbed into the black trans am left behind after the arrest. She was lucky Shanna left the keys in the ignition when everything went down.

She slid into the front driver's seat and pulled down the sun visor, checking her blue lipstick and reapplying for the next victim.

It was completely silent during the drive down the highway. Buildings flew by as she drove further into the city. Her last victim was located in the heart of town, only a few blocks away from her father.

She pulled up to the side of the road, the last victim's house just around the block. Climbing out, she made her way across the street, bag over her shoulder. There was a little convenience store there, still open, and as she walked by, she saw her face on the TV screen that hung in a corner.

She froze and watched. No, it wasn't her; it was Shanna, but the headline read differently. There was an alert, dangerous person abroad, call with any information regarding her whereabouts and do not engage.

They were only using Shanna's image, she must have told them.

Her eyes darkened with anger. She didn't have time to take care of the last victim anymore. She turned on her heels and marched down the sidewalk towards his house. That's okay, she thought. I'll make time. It wasn't long before she came upon his house, and, lucky for her, he was already asleep.

She walked to the front door and inspected it, an old-fashioned lock, no deadbolt. He was making this too easy for her. Pulling out her lock pick set from her back, she set to work. Coaxing the pick around the inside of the doorknob, listening for the telltale click to let her know she was hitting all the right spots. She gently applied pressure with the tension wrench, keeping the pins in place as she moved them.

It didn't take long before she was able to turn the lock all the way over, giving her access to the inside of the house. With a smug look on her face, she walked in, immediately assaulted by the surrounding mess. He drank a lot, and smoking was apparent from the smell that invaded the home. She didn't have to go far to find him, he was spread out in a reclined chair in the living room; the TV having shut itself off long ago.

She stood over him for a moment, taking in his disheveled appearance. Brown hair and untrimmed beard, a slight rumbling as he breathed in. It only angered her more. She pulled the case with the syringe and drugs out of her bag and held it up to the faint light of the moon outside the window. It didn't hurt to make sure she had the right dosage.

She shouldn't have to worry about his wife walking in on her. If she remembers correctly, he let it slip during his last session that she had already moved out. Living with her sister down the street apparently until she could afford a lawyer.

Gently placing the needle against the inside of her victim's elbow, she applied pressure and slipped the needle into his skin.

A groan escaped his lips, and he moved his head to the side.

The girl let out a sigh. She hated the unknown and you could never tell if someone was a light sleeper or not. Lucky for her the alcohol always helps. She reached, making her way to the rope, tying it off so she could tighten it around his neck. The drugs were going to do the job for her. After all, she made sure to give a big enough dose. However, she still needed the rope in place. Just for effect. Sending all of them the same message she had been sending since the beginning.

Reaching into her bag, she pulled out a little compact mirror and a tube of lipstick. She applied one more layer and checked her lipstick in the mirror one last time before the compact shut with a click.

She waited a moment longer for the drugs to take effect. The last thing she needed right now was him waking up on her while she put the noose around his neck. Not caring for subtlety anymore, she lifted his head and slipped the rope over the top. She grimaced at touching his hair, slightly wet from sweating in his sleep, and leaned down to place the kiss on his cheek.

There. Done.

Giving the noose one last tug to tighten it a bit. She felt for a pulse and, satisfied there wasn't one; she pushed the body up slightly at an angle. Her marker glided across his skin as she wrote "Judas" across the now dead man's back. Then, dropping the body with a small thud, she turned to pack up her equipment. Just enough left to take care of her father. Standing with her bag in hand, she headed to the door and walked out, not caring to shut it behind her even. She was officially in a hurry now. All she had left was her father and she couldn't risk getting caught before then. This was the entire purpose, after all.

With his house only being a couple blocks away, she didn't bother returning to the trans am. It was hard to believe the struggle she had to go through to get an address for him. Considering the circumstances, she thought this would make these things a little easier to find. But, apparently if the victims aren't under 18, they don't bother releasing addresses for public warnings about perverts like him.

She marched down the sidewalk, holding her arms tight across her body to fight off the chill of the wind, and made her way towards his house. He's been out for a few days now and should be settled nicely at home. Besides, he had a curfew being on parole. Not that the few small precautions the system does put in place are anywhere near enough. But at least it should guarantee him to be home. Her hair blows across her face as her walk quickens.

Chapter 31

There was no other vehicle in the driveway when they arrived and all the lights in the house were off. It was an older building, probably at least 50 years old. The outside walls probably used to be white but have long since been stained a dirty brown. Some vines grew up the side, wrapping themselves around the gutter, which was full of leaves.

"You sure we're at the right place?" Jane attempted to peek in through a dirty window and huffed when it proved impossible.

"Well, this is the address he had on file at the prison." Sean stomps up the front steps, each one creaking underfoot.

"Maybe he moved? Would his parole officer have the updated address?" Jane pulls out her cell phone and holds it in her hands, prepared to find out.

Sean nods, "Probably. But look..." He points down at an old faded doormat.

Jane follows his eyes with her own. The welcome mat, made of an old and worn out rubber, had obviously been there for years. Whatever color it used to be was completely gone, leaving just patches of pieces that weren't black as a tire. But what had caught Sean's eye about it was the holes in it. Small punctures in the mat keeping a left right pattern all the way across. It was obvious they were made by some kind of stiletto or high heel shoe. And probably fairly recently for the impressions to still be there.

"You thinking what I'm thinking?" Sean mutters, pulling his gun and holding it carefully by his side with both hands.

"This is our suspect's house?" Jane glances around somewhat anxiously but leaves her gun holstered rather than following her partner's lead. Noticing him nod she whispers, "but I doubt she's here. If she's after her dad, who obviously doesn't live here anymore and Shanna is in custody..."

Suddenly Sean's cell phone buzzes from his pocket. He jumps a little, startled, letting go of his gun with one hand and using it to slide his phone up to his ear.

"Captain?..... Yeah, we figured that out..... No, not yet. I was just about to..... Judge Mayflower..... Yes, sir. Bye."

He slides his gun back into his holster and begins typing frantically on his phone. Jane raises an eyebrow and leans forward, trying to see over his shoulder.

"Was Marshall confirming it's the suspect's house instead of the victims?" She questions softly.

"Yeah. Shanna told him." He mutters, continuing his typing.

"So we should go in and see if there's any clue to where he lives now and where she's going? I mean, we don't have a lot of time, right? Shouldn't we hurry?" Jane gestures at the door, practically bouncing in place.

"We need a warrant. I'm working on getting one now." He hits the last button and then stares at his phone in silence.

"Would this not be considered an exigent circumstance? I mean, we have a freaking serial killer on the loose! A man's life is in danger!" She's almost shouting now and Sean gives her a frustrated look.

"Unfortunately no. I agree it's ridiculous, but we could get fired..."

"I feel like a man's life might be worth that risk, but okay. You're the boss. How long will it..." the words weren't even completely out of her mouth when his phone buzzed with an email notification.

"That's it! Let's go!" Sean slips his phone back in his pocket and pulls his gun back up. He twists the doorknob and pushes it open, rushing in with Jane hot on his heels.

~~~~~

The inside of the house is spotless. Old, but clean. Jane expected dust and rust, but it would seem Shanna and her sister were pretty good at keeping things tidy.

'Maybe they practiced their crime scene clean ups at home first...' Jane thought with a smirk.

In the living room is an old couch, white and clean to the touch with a skirted bottom like one of the couches her grandma would have owned. In front of the couch sits a TV stand, but no TV on it. Everything is pretty outdated, as if they hadn't updated their furniture in at least a decade, but painted white and kept clean. Granted, that's when their dad went to prison, so maybe they haven't had a chance to buy new. The only thing in the house that hadn't been painted white was the old, dark hardwood floors.

There are also some nails in the walls as if pictures used to be hung there, but it's apparent they haven't been in quite some time. Jane briefly wonders what happened to the girl's mom... Maybe she'd look into that later, after they deal with the issue at hand, of course. She then makes her way to the kitchen, where she finds Sean.

The kitchen has recently been used. It smells of fruit and there are a few dishes drying on the rack. Sean goes to walk past her, touching her arm gently as he scoots through the small space between her and the stove. She shivers slightly at his touch, but he doest seem to notice. She watches as he disappears up the stairs.

Once he is gone, Jane starts opening drawers in the kitchen out of curiosity. Silverware in one, cookbooks in another, plates, cups. Nothing of importance. She makes her way to a room next to the kitchen and notices the bookshelves and desk inside. An office. Sitting down at the desk, she opens up the drawers, filing through some envelopes and papers inside.

Unfolding one of the papers, she scans it up and down. It's a receipt from the energy company. Looking at the back payments, it would seem they paid their bill in cash at the same time each month, almost to the day.

She tosses it aside and picks up the next one. This one is an envelope with a few things inside. Dumping it on the desktop, she rifles through the items, spreading them out to see them all clearly. Birth certificates, social security cards, and a few childhood medical records, it would seem. Jane grabs the birth certificates and thumbs through them quickly.

Steve Aaron Michaels
December 15th 1976
Leah Marie Smith
May 30th 1979
Shanna Erin Michaels
March 22nd 1997
Dinah Marie Michaels
March 22nd 1997

"Well... now we know the sisters' real name." Jane mutters to herself as she places everything back in the envelope and sets it with the energy receipt. She grabs the next paper and immediately jumps up out of her chair, still reading.

"Sean!" she shouts. Upstairs she can hear her partner's footsteps thudding against the floor and down the steps. He busts into the office nearly in a sweat, gun raised, finger on the trigger and ready.

Jane glances up at him in a moment of confusion and then realizes what she did. "Oh, sorry... didn't mean to scare you... I just found something."

Sean's face drops in a heavy sigh of both relief and frustration as he lowers his gun and slides it back into its holster.

"What's that?" He asks, nodding at the paper in her hand as she holds it up proudly.

"A confirmation of mail forwarding. It looks like someone, either Shanna or her sister, whose name is Dinah apparently by the way, went in and conned the post office into giving them the forwarding address for Michaels." Jane waves the paper around like she's just struck gold, but Sean moans.

"That means she could already be on her way there now. If not already there! We've got to get moving!" Sean turns on his heel and runs for the door. Jane chases after him with the address.

Leaping in the car, Sean drives this time. Jane spouts off the address as Sean turns on the lights.

"No siren?" Jane questions.

"Not today. Don't want her to hear us coming and speed up. We're already going to be lucky to make it in time. Radio for backup. Tell them no sirens."

"On it." Jane grabs for the radio as Sean peels out of the driveway, wheels throwing gravel behind them. "Oh, what was upstairs?"

Sean glances over at her just briefly before returning his eyes to the road. He lets go of the wheel with his right hand and reaches into his pants pocket. "A closet full of dresses, a vanity table, and this." He pulls out a small sandwich bag containing a tube of red lipstick and tosses it to her, returning his hand to the wheel.

She holds it up in her hand to look in at it closer. "Wanna bet that's going to be a match?"

"My thoughts exactly."

Chapter 32

"Shanna?" Steve stood in his kitchen, a glass of water in his hand. His brows drew together as he stared at the beautiful blonde woman in front of him. He set his glass of water down as realization slowly dawned on his face. "Dinah. Wha-what are you doing here?"

Dinah watched him as he cleared his throat, playing with his water on the countertop.

"It's like, 2 in the morning." He said as he glanced around, finding the time on the stovetop.

"How, how did you.." He turned and looked back towards Dinah, eyes drawing together as his voice trailed off.

Her voice rang clear through the kitchen space. "I wanted to visit you."

The corner of his mouth twitched a bit as he let out a nervous laugh. "Yeah?" He said. He ran his hand through the stubble on his face as he stared at his daughter.

She stared back, taking in how much he had aged. He looked like a different person. His beard had gone completely gray a long time ago and his hair, what little there was left, was following closely behind.

She hummed back an answer. Not really wanting to talk to him.

"Well." He said. "Do you wanna take a seat?" His arm jerked, pointing at a chair pushed up against a small table. "I don't have much right now......" He trailed off again. "Water?"

Dinah stared at the direction of the chair and only hummed again.

"How did you find me?" He asked.

She glanced down at the sound of a glass clinking against the counter in front of her. "I always know where you are. After all, you are my father."

He swallowed and shifted in place. "Okay." Seeming to gain a bit of confidence, he cleared his throat. "It's two in the morning. Couldn't you have come at a better time?"

Dinah swirled the water in the cup around, disinterested in the conversation. "I could have, but now was the best time."

"Why is that?" He asked.

"Time's running out."

"For what?"

She glanced at him. "That doesn't matter right now." She said, "Why did you do it?"

"Do what?"

"You know what." Her voice darkened as she stared. "You know she killed herself."

He looked down into his glass of water. Not answering. Whether because he didn't want to or he couldn't,

Dinah didn't care. She took a step closer to him, closing the gap between the two.

"It's your fault." She said, her voice barely above a whisper. This close to him, he seemed so small from what she remembered as a child. Insignificant.

"I know." He still couldn't meet her eyes.

"Do you really know?" She pulled out the syringe of medicine and held it up for him to see.

He finally looked up, eyeing the liquid inside. "What's that?"

"It's an antipsychotic." She answered. "Did you know they prescribed it to Shanna a few years back? She was going through a lot."

"Do you take it too?"

She looked away from the syringe and at him. "Who said she took it?"

Before he could register what she was saying, she stuck the needle in the side of his arm, depressing the syringe.

"What are you doing?" Steve jerked back, grabbing at the needle and pulling it out. He threw it to the floor and met Dinah's eyes. "What.."

"You only have a few minutes before it takes effect. I had to up the dose since I couldn't use a vein, but it'll still get the job done." She took steps towards him as he backed away.

"What job?"

"It's been a long time coming. I had a hard time waiting, so we had a few practice rounds. Ended up for the better cause now there are fewer men like you in this world."

"W-what?" He backed away even quicker. She didn't have to say much more for him to finally understand what was going on. "To your own father?" He let out a short bark of laughter. Putting even more distance between the two.

She looked him up and down, appearing to think about what he said.

He took this moment to turn and run, racing down the hallway towards his bedroom.

"It's too late to do anything now. The drug is already in your system."

He heard her voice echoing through the hallway. He struggled at the door, his hands already working against him.

Dinah stood at the end of the hallway and watched him. "It's your fault that I have to do this." She said, "If you had just been good."

"You're crazy!" He screamed at her, the door finally giving way and swinging open.

"No. I think I'm quite sane, actually." She followed his footsteps into his room. "Noone else sees it, but this has to be done. Think about how wonderful the world will be. Perfect, if we disposed of men like you."

Steve scrambled on the floor, his muscles going weak, unable to hold him up anymore. His hands digging underneath the mattress of his bed.

"Are you looking for something?" She asked.

"Did you really think I'd go down without a fight?" He responded, pulling a small pistol from under the mattress.

When Dinah saw him fumbling with the gun, she couldn't help but giggle.

Steve froze in place when he heard her laughter peeling through the room. "What's so funny?"

"It's true you can't fix a rotten apple, huh?" She reached down and picked the gun from his hands. He struggled against her. Quickly losing all control of his body.

He couldn't move any more at this point except to jerk, his leg lashing out hitting the nightstand. A crash sounded out as the lamp fell and hit the floor but Dinah ignored it, inspecting the gun in her hand.

"You're not supposed to have this. Besides, you can't even move to use it anymore."

Steve responded, his words incoherent mumbles.

She looked down at him. "Don't worry. This isn't how I'm going to kill you." She squatted down to his level. "You see, what's going to happen is I'm going to hang you. I think I'll do it while you're still conscious, too. So you can understand what's happening as you die."

He lay propped against the bed, unable to move or speak. Fear was written in his eyes as drool worked its way out of the corner of his mouth.

Dinah watched it, scrunching her nose at the sight, "Disgusting."

At that moment, she heard the front door burst open and footsteps in the kitchen.

She stood and sighed. "I need to take care of this first." She looked at the gun in her hand and made her way into the kitchen where the sound came from.

Chapter 33

It was around one o'clock in the morning when the judge's phone went off, waking him. He reached over and grabbed it off the nightstand, pressing his thumb down on the button to unlock the screen.

"Again?" the soft voice mumbled from behind him and he sighed, sitting up on the edge of the bed. He glanced back at his wife, her eyes still shut but clearly awake, given her question.

"I'm afraid so. I'll take it to the study. Sorry. Go back to sleep." He places the phone to his ear and marches out of the bedroom and down the hall.

"Didn't I just sign a warrant a few hours ago?..... Oh. They did?..... So now they...? Oh. Yes. Of course." The judge glances down at his desk. The picture of his wife and son sits smiling up at him. His stomach twists into a knot. This case brings back some terrible memories. "Yes, I understand. Email it to me and I'll sign it right away. Good luck." The phone beeps, letting him know the captain had hung up.

The judge sits down at his computer to wait for the warrant information to appear in his email. He's ready to be done with this case. Hopefully, it'll all be over after tonight.

~~~~~

They had screeched to a stop in front of the duplex moments earlier, and Jane had immediately leapt from the car. She had raced up the sidewalk only to suddenly have her arm yanked backwards. Having her momentum suddenly interrupted caused her arm to release a tingling sensation. Probably going to be a pulled muscle when the adrenaline wears off.

"Jane, hold up! We have to wait for the warrant!" Sean glances down at his grip on her arm and releases it. But he keeps his arm outstretched, as a continued warning.

"Again?!" she asks.

"You know the law..." He said. His voice comes out in a soft whisper. It's clear from his body language that he's nervous. He doesn't like the situation either.

Jane lifts her head to the sky and lets out an exasperated moan before looking back at her partner again. "She's in there right now. Possibly in the middle of killing him! And we're supposed to just... sit out here and let it happen?"

Sean lowers his arm and huffs. He crunches his shoes into the gravel as he thinks.

"We can go up to the door and listen. But Jane, I'm serious. We cannot go in without a warrant or probable cause." He responded.

She contemplates this for a moment and then sighs, holding her arm out to suggest her partner take the lead. He passes her and she falls in step behind him.

Outside the front door, they listen carefully. Sean presses his head against the door as Jane tries to peek through the window. The blinds are in the way and she can't see anything but a line of wall and ceiling.

"Hear anything?" She asks anxiously.

"No. Maybe... I don't know. Nothing definitive." He said. He glances up at her and she raises an eyebrow. "Nothing that would justify bursting in without a warrant. If that was going to be your next question."

"Ugh!" Jane groans and her partner shushes her, so she lowers her voice slightly. "I just can't stand this anymore! He could be dying right now and..." she said.

Sean sticks his hand up, and she goes silent. He pulls out his phone, glances at the screen, and then shoves it back in his pocket and nods.

"Did we get it?" She's practically bouncing now.

"Yeah, we got it." He responded.

"So let's go!" She tries to push past him and he blocks her path. "What now?!" she huffs.

"Backup is on the way... What if this gets messy? Maybe we should wait for help..."

"There's no time for that! Sean! We have to help him!" She gestures to the door in frustration.

Sean sighs and nods. "I think there's a back door. Maybe we should split up and come from both sides. We don't know what the situation is in there and that way maybe we at least get her cornered..."

Jane thinks about it for a moment and agrees. There would be less chance of her escaping that way. And they don't want to risk putting the family on the other side of the duplex at risk either. "Okay, let's do it." She said.

"I'll go around back. When I get there, I'll whistle. That's when we move in..." Before Jane can respond, Sean is bolting off around the side of the building.

~~~~~

Halfway around the building, Sean spots a wooden fence.

"Seriously?!" He growls. "That's a fire hazard..."

He walks up to the fence and gauges how difficult it would be to climb over. Grabbing the top of the fence, he goes to pull himself up.

"This is not okay..." groaning, he manages to pull himself up and lay across the top of the fence. He glances over to make sure there's nothing in the way for him to slide on over. The back alley has a dumpster not far off and some trash cans. A few puddles of muddy water lay here and there and a mouse or two scurries by. It's still dark out, but the glow coming from behind the building allows enough light for him to see. The back porch light must be on...

Sliding down off the top of the fence, Sean winces as he feels a small splinter dig into his arm. As he lands, he inspects his arm before glancing around again.

'Why do they have garbage cans and a dumpster back here if they've got it fenced off, anyway? How can anybody even get back here to remove it?' As he's contemplating that thought, there's a crash from inside the window near his head and he ducks instinctively. That must be the room she's in... He tries to peer in the window inconspicuously, but it's too high above his head. So he continues around the side of the building, looking for the back door.

~~~~~

It's taking Sean a lot longer to get back there than Jane expected it to...

'Maybe I should go after him... What if something happened to him?' she paces nervously. 'We don't really have time for this... what if...'

Before she can finish the thought, there's a loud crash inside the duplex. She whips out her gun and holds it up, preparing for the worst. But nothing else happens. 'Was that probable cause? I mean... we already have the warrant... Where is Sean?'

Jane runs her fingers through her hair anxiously and moans. 'That's it... I've got to do something... I can't just sit here any longer...'

She slams her body against the door, forcing it open. As she stumbles into a living area, she lifts her gun and turns side to side, surveying her surroundings. Everything's quiet as she listens, trying to figure out which direction in the house she needs to go. There's a long hallway to her left and down it she can hear what sounds like a soft voice.

"... care of this first"

Soft footsteps make their way across the hall, and Jane rushes across the room to hide behind the corner at the opening of the hallway. A bullet whizzes past her head, just barely missing her. She sighs with relief as she dives behind the corner, only to feel a burning sensation in her right calf.

As she lands on the floor behind the corner, she yanks her leg behind the wall. It takes everything in her not to scream as she looks down at her torn pant leg and the blood pouring from it.

"This can't be happening..." she cringes. She leans ever so slightly around the corner, catching a glimpse of some shiny blonde hair whipping back around the edge of the back bedroom door. Jane fires a round that skims the bedroom door frame but doesn't make contact with Dinah. To be honest, she knew it wouldn't hit her, but Jane wanted to make it clear that just because she's been hit doesn't mean she's easy prey.

A very feminine yet sinister voice echoes down the hall, "You're ruining everything you know?"

"Well, you aren't exactly making my life easy either, honey."

Jane rests her head against the wall behind her and looks up at the ceiling. 'Why didn't I wait for Sean?'

~~~~~

Sean's heart nearly stopped when he heard the gunshots start. He had just spotted the back door ahead when he heard them and hit the ground. At first, he thought maybe she had seen him outside the window and was targeting him. But no, the gunshots were coming from inside the building.

A gun isn't usually Dinah's MO...

So why would....

He gasps, 'oh no'... "Jane!"

He races to the back door, but it's locked. He can't shoot the metal of the doorknob or the bullet may ricochet, so he resorts to kicking the door in. It takes several good hits before splintering and busting open.

The room before him appears to be a laundry room. It's cramped, barely enough space between the washer and dryer and the wall in front of them. Sean squeezes through as quick as he can, gun held high, not sure what to expect.

He flings the laundry room door open and rushes through. The kitchen. His eyes dart around, searching for danger.

"Making my life easy either, honey." The sound of Jane's voice sends an instant flood of relief through Sean's body. He heads in her direction. After rounding the corner at the end of the kitchen, he can see the front door and, about 10 ft down from him, leaned up against another wall was Jane.

'Why is she on the floor?' fear grips him as he tries to get a good look at his partner without becoming a target himself. His eyes scan her from head down. She has sweat matted to her head already, but as he got down to her legs, he saw the problem. There's a small pool of blood under her right leg. It's not enough to be coming from an artery, but it doesn't look good either.

"Dang it Jane..." He mutters under his breath in frustration. 'Why didn't she wait for me?'

"Pssst..." Sean tries to get her his partner's attention. "Pssst..."

Finally, after a few attempts, she looks at him. Her face just washes over with relief upon seeing him and any anger he had towards her is instantly gone. His only goal now is getting her out safely.

Chapter 34

Dinah made her way back into the bedroom, shutting and locking the door behind her. "I don't have time for this." She said, turning to look at her father, who laid across the floor, unable to move. Drool running down the side of his mouth, leaving Dinah with a churning in her gut.

She pulled her tools out of the bag she carried with her and proceeded to set up what was needed. She didn't have time for the pulley system she and Shana would normally use, so she went with the next best thing. The pole in his closet.

"Here daddy dearest, I think this will look good on you." She smirked at him and placed the noose around his neck, pulling tight. The rough frays of the rope scraping against her bare hands.

The sound of shuffling feet made its way down the hallway, pausing her advances again.

Dinah sighed, "If she doesn't stop interfering, I may have to do away with her as well." She spoke to her father even though he couldn't respond.

She peeked through the bedroom door, seeing movement near the kitchen at the end. A crack sounded through as she fired a shot in their direction. A quick yelp came from the female and there was a blur as someone disappeared behind a wall again.

Dinah scowled at the movement. There were two of them now. She had her hands full. She shut the bedroom door again, returning to her work.

"Turn yourself in, Dinah. Your sister's already told us everything!" A male voice yelled out down the hallway.

She drug her father across the floor by the rope attached to him. Gurgling sounds could be heard coming from the back of his throat as the rope dug in.

The bedroom door splintered open when a shot fired.

"You're messing everything up!" Dinah yelled. She was increasingly getting frustrated at the interruptions and wanted to get this over with.

She dropped the rope and fired two more shots down the hallway, not caring for the door anymore.

"Sean, are you okay?" The female officer hissed in a half whisper.

"Fine." His reply was curt.

Dinah proceeded to slip the rope around the pole and pull, dragging Steve's body along with it. He was pulled into a sitting position, suspended by the noose digging into his neck. Dinah locked eyes with him as she gave another yank on the rope. His face was going a deep crimson as he gurgled more against his restraints.

His eyes bulged from the pressure, bloodshot and fear screaming through them.

She stared back, savoring every moment. This is what she lived for, the very thing she dreamt about every night for the past ten years.

Sean's voice broke through her senses, interrupting the thrill that ran through her. "Dinah, talk to me." Shuffling came from the direction of his voice. "He's your father. I know he did bad things, but he doesn't deserve this."

One hand still on the rope, the other grasping the gun, she turned and aimed it at the gaping hole in the doorway. "You know nothing." She fired another shot, keeping the officers at bay.

The female officer gave an uneasy sound. "Sean, be careful." Her voice was strained.

"It's okay, Jane, I'm just talking to her." He spoke back. His voice was soft as he spoke to her.

A strangled gag filled the silence as Dinah jerked on the rope, pulling Steve higher off the ground.

Sean called out, speaking with urgency, "I do know. He raped and killed a girl. Thrown into prison for years and left you alone with your sister."

Dinah groaned in annoyance. "I told you. You. Know. Nothing!" Her voice rose in pitch. She could feel herself slipping and closed her eyes, gaining her composure.

"Then tell me." Sean's voice floated through the hallway.

Dinah pulled harder on the rope. Even putting her weight into it, she could only get him inches off the floor. "I don't have to tell you anything." She gritted between her teeth, watching as Steve's eyes fluttered and his face turned an alarming shade of purple. At the rate she was going, the drugs would beat her to him.

"Sean." Jane whispered, "Don't-"

"What about your mom? How do you think she would feel knowing what you've done?" Sean yelled out, his voice too close to the door.

The rope burned as it slipped through her fingers and her father's body slammed against the floor. She whipped around, her fingers white as she gripped the gun.

"Don't bring my mother into this!" She shook all over and her vision blurred. It was as if something snapped inside of her, releasing what lived deep inside of her. The barrel of the gun shook violently as she tried to aim at the door. "It's his fault she's dead! He killed her!"

"Our records say she killed herself." Jane sounded confused as she spoke to Sean, trying to keep her voice down.

"Your *records* are wrong!" Dinah's jaw clenched. "He's the reason she died that night. She couldn't bear the thought of what others would say! How they would look at us!" she screamed. "He broke her! Beat her and broke her!"

Tears threatened at the edges of her eyes, and her heart thrummed against her chest. She was frustrated. Angry at the officers for thinking her mother killed herself. Her hands continued to shake with the gun held tightly between her fingers. She needed to let it out, to kill someone, and right now the officer, Sean, was looking perfect.

She stepped in front of the door and Sean's face was directly level with the barrel of her gun. Hands still shaking and her knuckles white, she stood still. Sean's gun was pointed at her. Calm and unmoving.

"You don't have the right to speak about my mother." Her voice stilted through clenched teeth.

"Put the gun down and we can make this easy." He soothed.

She wavered for only a moment. "He has to die."

Sean's eyes stayed focused on Dinah, leaving no opening. He was relaxed as he held his stance, taking in her strained appearance. "That was smart. What you did."

Dinah scrunched her eyebrows, taken aback at the sudden change in conversation.

"Judas, I mean. He hung himself because he betrayed Jesus." He held her gaze. "Your dad betrayed your mom. And you. Right?"

"So did the others. They all betrayed their wives." She stared back at the officer in front of her. What was he doing?

"That's creative. The others didn't get it at first."

"But you did?" She asked.

"Yeah." He let out a dry chuckle. "I think my boss suspected me at first."

A flash of light shone through the windows, blinding Dinah. She dropped the gun to guard her face as the room lit up like daylight. Rough hands grabbed her wrists and threw her to the ground. She struggled against his grip as the cool metal of cuffs locked closed and trapped her.

Sean's voice spoke through the sounds of footsteps rushing through the home as it flooded with uniformed men and women. It was hard and cold. "You have the right to remain silent."

Chapter 35

As soon as Sean hands Dinah off to S.W.A.T, he rushes to find Jane. She had insisted the other officers go straight in to help him, so when he finds her she was still on the floor, trying her best to pull herself up the wall. He darts towards her and catches her just before she falls back down. Swooping his arms underneath her, Sean lifts his partner off her feet and into his firm embrace.

As he carries her, he can hear the ambulance sirens coming up on the scene. Just in time. He glances down at Jane's face as he twists sideways through the open door with her. She looks tired… probably from the blood loss.

"I would have gotten up on my own eventually, you know." She gives him a weak smile, and he returns it.

"You could just say thanks."

"I'm not complaining. I've been trying to get in your arms for a while now."

"I think there might have been a better way." He shakes his head in amusement, glancing around to make sure nobody is close enough to hear them.

As they come upon the ambulance, the EMTs are already opening the back hatch and pulling out a gurney. Sean gently places his partner down on one and steps back so the EMTs can do their job.

"I'll meet you at the hospital, okay?" Sean calls out to Jane as the doors close behind her. Another ambulance pulls up and Sean watches as they place Steve Michaels on the gurney unconscious. The solemn look on the medics faces tells him all he needs to know about his chances. Sean grimaces and begins marching to his vehicle.

Suddenly, a well-dressed man with a shiny gold badge dangling from a chain around his neck steps in front of him. Sean's eyes drift down to the badge and he grinds his teeth.

FBI.

"Detective Fenton?"

"Here to steal the credit, are you?" Sean mutters as he attempts to go around the agent before him. Unfortunately, the man blocks his path yet again.

Sean sighs. "What?"

"Good work on this case. We're told you and your partner were instrumental in this being closed as quickly as it was." The man held his hand out, but Sean just looked at it.

"Three weeks and eight bodies is quickly to you?"

"You know serial offender cases can take months or even years. To close this out in under a month IS great work. Just accept the compliment." The man frowns, annoyed.

"Thanks. Now, if you don't mind, I need to get to the hospital. My partner was shot. In case you weren't aware."

"We're aware. But we'd like to talk to you about taking a job with us at the bureau here in New York."

"Not interested."

Now the man looks extra frustrated. "You haven't even heard me out yet."

"Don't need to. I'm happy where I am. Well... At least with the agency I'm with." Sean attempts to push past the man again and the agent actually scoots aside a bit. But as Sean goes to pass by, the agent responds again.

"What about your partner, then?"

Sean pauses. He considers this a moment and then shrugs. "You'd have to ask her."

Then he climbs in his vehicle and peels out of the cul-de-sac, speeding towards the hospital.

~~~~~

The monitor next to Jane's hospital bed beeped. It had been doing that repetitively since she'd woken up. Apparently, the bullet had passed straight through her leg, so there was no need for a removal surgery. After some minor stitching on the exit wound and some gauze and tape on the entrance wound and the doctors had left her alone to rest.

The two needles in her arm are uncomfortable, and she tries her best to avoid looking at them. A figure appears in the doorway and she looks up with a grin.

"Took you long enough."

Her partner gives a soft smile and makes a beeline for her. "Got held up by the feds. And traffic. I think I prefer traffic."

She laughs, "You would."

"Me? And here I thought you were the one who didn't trust people." Sean takes her hand and strokes it with his thumb. It sends a little sensation up her wrist.

"I guess I'm getting better at that. Opening myself up more." She looks into his eyes, trying to display everything with a look. Sean starts to open his mouth to say something and Jane's heart races. But then the curtain opens again and they both turn. Sean drops her hand as he twists around and leaps to his feet.

An FBI agent shuffles in, nodding at Sean before turning his attention to her. "Officer Matthews, good to see you awake and smiling. I'm agent Reed Davison from the New York division of the FBI. I was hoping to get a moment of your time if it's alright with your partner." The man glances at Sean and he nods.

"I've gotta go see about Michaels. I'll uh, check back in with you in a few?" Her partner's eyes meet hers again and she nods as if to give him permission to leave. Then he does, closing the curtain back behind him.

~~~~~

A small Hispanic woman in a white coat with a clipboard closes the curtain to Michael's room as she exits. Sean waves to get her attention as he skips up to her.

"Dr. Garcia?"

"Yes. Can I help you?" The woman looks up at him curiously and he pulls out his badge.

"Any update on our victim?"

"Unfortunately, there isn't a reversal for Quetiapine. We started pushing fluids as soon as he came in, but the best we can do in a case like this is a monitor for organ failure. And unfortunately, it looks like that's exactly what's happening. His liver is failing and his lungs aren't far behind. We don't have time to find a donor and even if we did, the damage is so extensive... Honestly, we're out of options here. He has maybe a day left, max." She sighs and gestures towards his room. "I doubt he'll be able to speak much through the pain, but he's awake if you're needing a statement. You're welcome to try."

"Thank you." Sean nods at her and pushes through the curtain into the room.

Steve has wires and tubes going in every direction. There's a soft moaning sound coming from deep in his throat, and Sean can't help but feel a pang of responsibility. If he'd just been a few minutes quicker. Maybe there'd be less yellow tape if they didn't always have to wait for the red tape first... Now he's starting to sound like Jane. He shakes his head and tries not to think about it.

"Steve Michaels?"

The man opens his eyes and glances at Sean. There's pain in them.

"Mr. Michaels, are you able to answer a few questions? You don't have to speak. I can ask yes or no questions if I need to." Sean sits down in an empty chair by the bed and pulls out a notebook.

Michaels looks at him sadly, "Di...Dine..."

"She's alive. She'll be charged."

Tears stream down his face. "My fault..." he chokes out. It's not a question. Sean isn't sure how to respond, so he just stays quiet. Michaels continues, "I want... I'm... sorry."

Sean puts the notebook away. He can tell there's no point in trying to get a statement and really it won't matter. But it's obvious there's something useful he can do for this man.

"Sir, would you like to have me call a priest or someone for you?"

Steve's eyes glisten, giving off a glimmer of hope, and Sean doesn't need a verbal answer to understand. "I'll do that right now."

Chapter 36

"Dinah, please consider this. It may very well be the only way to lessen your sentence." A dark-haired investigator, Ms. Cynthia from the Public Defender's Office, as she had introduced herself earlier, stared across the table at Dinah. Her voice was clear and melodic, the type of voice that commanded attention in a courtroom.

Dinah maintained eye contact. The investigator's brown eyes never wavered. She watched Dinah lounge back in her seat, her leg crossed over one knee and one finger tapping a slow rhythm against her thigh.

"The psychiatrist has determined that you have ASPD with a strong case of OCD and that can place you in a suitable position to at least not be given capital punishment. You could be looking at a life sentence. Depending on the judge and if you agree to take medication and receive psychiatric help, you may get an even lighter sentencing."

Cynthia continued to make a case for the woman sitting across from her. She had been briefed on the situation beforehand and was attempting to get the cooperation of her client so that the attorneys could do their job.

Dinah's face showed no signs that she was going to respond. She continued to tap her finger against her leg, almost in a soothing manner.

Cynthia sat back away from the table and let out a slow sigh. "Shanna has already decided to use her diagnosis' to lessen her punishment, and she was hoping you would do the same." She glanced at Dinah to see if there was a reaction to her sister's name. "Her hearing is soon, and it's actually looking good for her. If you give us a chance to help, we hopefully could do the same for you as well."

Dinah's finger went still, just resting in its place. The silence in the room was deafening, and the investigator adjusted herself in her seat. The stark fluorescent bulbs in the room and the roaring of silence were unsettling. Especially knowing that one of the two women sitting in the room was a killer. And enjoyed it.

The investigator cleared her throat, an attempt to break the silence and the unease that was settling into the room. Even though Dinah was cuffed and there were guards stationed, her presence was still suffocating.

"Is he dead?"

Cynthia jumped a bit at the sudden loudness of a voice. She adjusted her blazer and sat up straight in her seat. Hiding how startled she was. "You mean Mr. Michaels?"

"Yes." Dinah's finger started tapping again. "Mr. Michaels." She whispered his name, as though she didn't want to say it to begin with.

Cynthia nodded to herself more than to Dinah as she responded. "Yes, he passed not long after being taken to the hospital."

A smirk played at the edges of Dinah's lips and she uncrossed her legs, sitting up straighter. "Good."

The investigator clenched her jaws and bit back the retort that climbed the back of her throat. She had to remind herself that the young woman sitting in front of her was the reason for multiple deaths. With the goal of killing her own father.

"Tell me how you wish to go about this, Dinah. We need to make a decision today." Cynthia messed with her papers, placing them in order, if only to distract her from her own thoughts.

"I don't care what they rule. I've done my job." She responded.

"What of your sister? She was hoping you would plead insanity." Cynthia took notes in her file on Dinah's decision.

"I could care less what she wants or does." Dinah leaned forward and braced her elbows on the table. A slow smile creeped across her face. "I'm not insane. I knew exactly what I was doing."

The investigator's grip on her pen tightened, and she jotted down what Dinah said. After a moment, she closed her file and stood up, things in hand. "Very well, then. I guess the next time we will see each other will be in the courtroom."

Cynthia's heels clicked across the floor as she left the room, turning only briefly to see Dinah's cuffed hand in the air, fingers wiggling. "Bye bye." She said, grinning.

The group of twelve slowly made their way back to the jurors' box. The panel was split evenly, male to female. Not one of them appeared to want to be there. The group consisted of a couple of older women, dressed as though their clothes had been raided from a thrift store run by a colorblind 90-year-old grandmother. One had dark, tightly coiled hair streaked with white that she kept in its natural state, the other's hair bright white and thinned to the point you could see through it. One woman had hair dyed bright neon green. Stark against the slacks and suit jacket she sported and behind her followed a young man, clean dressed in dark pants and a white button up.

A short stocky man who was balding on top took his seat next to them and two more men, one in his mid-forties and the other no older than twenty, followed behind. The last three women were in their mid-thirties in age and ranged in ethnicities. An older gentleman who walked with a slight limp was one of the last to sit down, the foreperson being the only one still standing.

The room was silent. The only sound was the creaking of chairs as they scraped across the floor and the weight of the Jurors sitting down. Her council sat around her waiting, just as the rest of the room was, for the verdict.

Dinah watched on. The panel was a group of mismatched people, but that was the purpose, she supposed. Not like their decision was hard. She told them everything they wanted to hear.

The court clerk, a stoutly built man, cleared his throat after they were all seated. "May the presiding juror deliver the verdict?" His deep voice filled the silent space of the courtroom.

The juror still standing, a middle-aged man with graying red hair and a slightly wrinkled powder blue shirt, nodded at the clerk. He ran the palms of his hands against his pants, wiping off the few nerves he had. He handed the written verdict over to the court clerk and takes his seat.

The clerk looked over the paper. "The jury has found the defendant guilty of 10 cases of first degree murders."

Judge Nichols, a newly appointed judge who still had an air of freshness and desire to uphold the law, turned to face the defending council. "Does the defending council wish to poll the jury?"

The dark-haired attorney sitting next to Dinah responded. "Yes."

Judge Nichols turned back to the panel and proceeded to question them individually. Each one answering yes. The last one to be questioned was the young girl with bright neon green hair. "Is this your verdict?"

She glanced at Dinah long enough to make eye contact before looking away. "Yes."

Epilogue

"So, how did your first meeting with Shanna go? Wasn't that yesterday?" Sean asks as Jane unbuckles her seatbelt.

"Yeah. I don't know. It's hard. I have to balance knowing what she's done with knowing what she's been through... I'm glad she pleaded insanity because of her BPD and that she's getting help instead of being executed. But I'm definitely struggling to overcome the urge to look at her like just a criminal and not a human being. I guess I've always struggled with that, though." Jane sighs and pushes the door open. Sean climbs out and walks around the car to meet her.

"Well, if it's any consolation, I think you've grown in that respect. And I mean, insane or not... She is a criminal. You've got to give yourself a little grace. You're handling this a lot better than most would. I think the fact that you volunteered to mentor her at all is a huge indicator of your desire to grow from this..." He takes her by the hand and she brushes her thumb along the side of his.

"Yeah, I know. I'm trying anyway." She gives him an appreciative grin and then glances up the steps before them at the open doors and the crowd of strangers chattering about. Her face changes briefly, giving away her slight discomfort at being where she is. Sean picks up on it.

"Thanks for coming with me." He gives Jane's hand a gentle squeeze, "I know this isn't your thing and all..."

"Of course." She grins awkwardly at him, obviously trying to appear reassuring, as he steps up the front stairs and into the church.

He still had her hand in his, even though he was a step or two ahead of her, so it almost felt like he was pulling her behind him. The thought made him slightly uncomfortable, and the moment they were through the door, he repositioned himself by her side. Granted, he could have always just let go of her hand... but honestly, feeling the warmth of her palm against his was helping calm his nerves. After all, this is the first time he's been in a church service in many years.

Brother Ben was just ahead, greeting everyone as they passed and shaking hands. Sean gestured with his head in his direction to Jane and she nodded back, understanding. They walk up to him and Brother Ben's eyes seem to light up. Releasing Jane's hand, Sean reaches out to shake the pastors.

"Sean! I'm glad you could make it. It's great to see you again!" Ben smiles warmly.

"Thanks, you too." Sean steps aside slightly revealing Jane behind him, "And this is my girlfriend and former partner, Jane."

"Nice to meet you, Jane! I'm the pastor here, but you're welcome to call me Brother Ben if you want.

Forgive me, but I'm a bit curious... Former partner?" He raises an eyebrow at Sean but it's Jane who responds.

"I've recently accepted a position elsewhere. It was a good career move and... well..." she grins at Sean and loops her arm through his.

"Ah, gotcha." The pastor smiles knowingly and nods. "Regulations state you can't date your partner, correct?"

"Exactly." Jane nods and brother Ben chuckles.

"Well congratulations. We're glad to have you with us today." They both nod and thank him, then Jane leaves them to go find a seat.

"Pastor... I'd like to thank you again for coming up to the hospital the other night to talk with Michaels. It seemed to give him a lot of peace." Sean's eyes water slightly as he remembers the look on the man's face as the pastor prayed with him and he had taken his dying breath.

"It was my pleasure. It's one of the hardest and most rewarding parts of my job." He places a hand on Sean's shoulder. "Feel free to call me anytime. I'm always happy to help with that."

"I'm going to assume they don't necessarily have to be on their deathbed for you to pray with them like that?" Sean clears his throat nervously, and the pastor smiles and narrows his eyes slightly.

"Your assumption would be correct. Any chance there's a specific reason you're asking?"

"Well..." Sean nods his head and smiles wide. "I suppose there is."

The End.

*"When Jesus had thus said, he was troubled in spirit, and testified, and said, Verily, verily, I say unto you, that one of you shall betray me. Jesus answered, He it is, to whom I shall give a sop, when I have dipped it. And when he had dipped the sop, he gave it to Judas Iscariot, the son of Simon. And after the sop Satan entered into him. Then said Jesus unto him, That thou doest, do quickly."
John 13:21, 26-27 KJV*

"When the morning was come, all the chief priests and elders of the people took counsel against Jesus to put him to death: And when they had bound him, they led him away, and delivered him to Pontius Pilate the governor. Then Judas, which had betrayed him, when he saw that he was condemned, repented himself, and brought again the thirty pieces of silver to the chief priests and elders, Saying, I have sinned in that I have betrayed the innocent blood. And they said, What is that to us? see thou to that. And he cast down the pieces of silver in the temple, and departed, and went and hanged himself. And the chief priests took the silver pieces, and said, It is not lawful for to put them into the treasury, because it is the price of blood. And they took counsel, and bought with them the potter's field, to bury strangers in. Wherefore that field was called, The field of blood, unto this day. Then was fulfilled that which was spoken by Jeremiah the prophet, saying, And they took the thirty pieces of silver, the price of him that was valued, whom they of the children of Israel did value; And gave them for the potter's field, as the Lord appointed me."

Matthew 27:1-10 KJV

"To do justice and judgment is more acceptable to the Lord than sacrifice."
Proverbs 21:3 KJV

"Dearly beloved, avenge not yourselves, but rather give place unto wrath: for it is written, Vengeance is mine; I will repay, saith the Lord. Be not overcome of evil, but overcome evil with good."
Romans 12:19, 21 KJV

"If we confess our sins, He is faithful and just to forgive us our sins, and to cleanse us from all unrighteousness."
1 John 1:9 KJV

Special thanks to Michael, Laura, and Mary for their help and advice during the research process.
Thanks to Kayla N. Todd: my amazing illustrator, co-author, and best friend.
Thanks also to all my readers and those who have supported me over the years.
And most importantly, thanks to my Lord and Savior: Jesus Christ. My salvation, my life, and my writing is all thanks to Him.
~Layla

www.ingramcontent.com/pod-product-compliance
Lightning Source LLC
LaVergne TN
LVHW021942060526
838200LV00042B/1897